When the Cuckoo Called

I0682361

Avilasha Sarmah

WORDIT ART FUND

This book has been fully funded by the Wordit Art Fund. Wordit Art Fund helps deserving authors publish their work by providing monetary support. To apply for funding, please visit us at www.BecomeShakespeare.com

First published in 2017 by
Becomeshakespeare.com
Wordit Content Design & Editing Services Pvt Ltd
Unit - 26, Building A-1, Nr Wadala RTO, Wadala (East),
Mumbai 400037, India
T:+91 8080226699

©
ISBN 978-93-86487-63-6

Editing by Paramita Sarma

DEDICATION

I would like to dedicate my book to all the wide-eyed
wanderers in the wilderness who dares to live
answering the call of their authentic selves!

PREFACE

"When the Cuckoo Called" is written in an unconventional manner, not chronologically, across time and through places. I have divided the book into four parts (chapters) and named it after the seasons depending on the mood of the theme. The story starts in **Autumn** staying true to the essence of the season of falling leaves and melancholy comfort and actually talks about the current phase in the lives of the protagonists. The second part goes back to the events of **Summer** and traces the energetic, feisty vibe of the past as is the season. The Third part is named **Winter** which expresses the cold and hibernating aura of almost endings. Finally there is **Spring,** a season of beginnings and a rejuvenation which follows winter as the story ends.

There are references to a few songs in the book. Since the story is based on several places, I have tried to maintain the indigenousness. I first started writing this book when I was 16 years old and it took me four years to arrive at a final draft. In many cultures, such as ours, in the North Eastern part of India, the call of the cuckoo bird symbolizes the onset of spring; I have used the same reference to name my book thus. Hope you find pleasure reading the tale of two individuals, in their journey of self exploration tracing music in their lyrics. It would be of my greatest achievement if as an author I am able to make the reader *feel* and introspect. Thank You.

Avilasha Sarmah.

ACKNOWLEDGMENTS

Thank you to my editor and aunt, Paramita Sarma for her relentless guide and motivation. I am indebted to my parents for their support all throughout and for believing in my unconventional ways. I am extremely grateful to all my friends and family for their constant encouragement and enthusiasm in my passion. I want to thank Malini Nair from Leadstart for the recommendation of my book to the Wordit Art Fund and an immense 'thank you' to the Wordit CDE for the great opportunity and for making me a part of the family. Most importantly, I am immensely thankful to my publisher the BecomeShakespeare.com for publishing my book and my entire project management team for their help and guidance. I am also grateful to my friend, Parth Ahuja, for letting me use his amazing photos for the cover. Thank you to my cover designer and illustrator for the cover design adding an enhanced essence to the book.

DISCLAIMER

This is a work of fiction. Names, characters, businesses, places, events and incidents are either the products of the author's imagination or used in a fictitious manner. Any resemblance to actual persons, living or dead, or actual events is purely coincidental.

CONTENTS

Autumn

I

The countryside, wrapped in a feel of exotica, looked like a picture out of a postcard. The sky was crimson, post sunset, as she drove down the highway, along the tree-lined avenue amidst wide green pastures, towards the horizon beckoning to a kingdom of beautifully crafted cloud-tinged mountains in the distance. Totally a scene out of a movie and one would expect the words "THE END" to pop out in the background as the picture fades to black, tuned to a happy electrically playful melody, perhaps a love song or even a high end musical number. But in this case, it wouldn't be so, because it seems this is just the beginning!

As the saying goes, "Everything in life has a beautiful ending, if it's not, be sure it's not the ending but just the beginning." Many a critic(s) may have conflicting ideas about this but it is possibly true. Fairytales never ended without one, neither do the present day lifelike movies, nor does any fictional work in good stead; even real people, every single one of us crave for a happy ending no matter the means, it is mere living after all.

In the current stance, the story is devoid of music, there are no dulcets harmonizing with the plot. But it isn't complete silence either, just mere random everyday sounds, the tinge of a 'reality vibe'. Some automobile rumblings and their beeps on the road, voices of people talking, low and high, perhaps a dog barking in the distance, a few cows mooing and the bleating of sheep grazing in the green fields in the vicinity and rarely, ever so subtly, even a birdsong, but never a cuckoo's call.. *Has the songbird abandoned its song?* So, like a fairytale upside –down this story unfolds.

....

The speeding minion yellow Volkswagen Beetle came to a halt before an old-fashioned house, with fading paint and barely hanging shutters, reminiscent of a weary old man who had been through life's crests and troughs and was now waiting for its end, looking forward to eternal rest after his fair share of life. The young woman who was driving it, got out of her car and headed straight for the front verandah with misshaped railings and a wooden reclining chair. A woman probably in her late fifties was already waiting for her, and hugged her tight as she approached. Then locking the blue front door, the woman carried her sole baggage and both walked down the steps towards the car. The girl took hold of the woman's hand as they reached the pretty little gate of the villa. The older woman stopped at the gate and turned around to cast a last look backwards as if to bid adieu to her weary old companion. Then they both got into the car and drove off.

This time around they were retreating into the beautiful scenery. Since it was already getting dark, most of the houses had put on their lights and it appeared as if they were little glow worms glistening in the dark. On the way back, the girl couldn't stop talking about her wedding. Her old nurse who had brought her up in childhood listened to her in wonder, love and adoration glowing in her eyes for the little girl whom she had cared for as a baby and who was not so little anymore. The girl had found her *prince charming*, she exclaimed and there cannot be anyone else! He was exactly what she had wanted and it was like a dream come true and she couldn't help rejoicing!

Driving along they reached a sleepy town with few shops, some eateries and a petrol pump. She slowed the car near a roadside stall where they ordered tea, which they sipped in little earthen cups, along with home-made coconut sweets. The city girl was quite delighted at the rustic air of the place and exclaimed in wonder at the whole ambience of it!

After a while, done with the refreshments, they resumed their journey hoping to reach the big city by nightfall.

****

Miles away, across continents and oceans, in a city immersed in lights where the tall buildings looked like light-houses and the picturesque countryside had no rustic feel to it, the 'People's Singer' as he called himself was preparing for his first show in Lancashire for the *Indians* residing there. That night, under the stars on the open air makeshift stage, he would be starting the first leg of his overseas tour. He was jubilant, but not completely. He should have been at the top of the world. He was slightly nervous, and no wonder beaming with joy but he felt nothing extraordinary.

His show started and he was welcomed with cheers by the people, most of them young Indians in their twenties like himself. At the same time, he even noticed quite a number of *foreign* faces in the crowd.

After a few sentences expressing thankfulness and shout-outs to the people accompanied by a swarming rock guitar in the background, he stared singing; first warming up with a couple of unreleased songs from his new album and then following with his most popular ones. His was a different kind of music, unlike what was the trend in India. It was a mixture of genres; a touch of country tuned to rock music, hence the use of both electric guitar and his rendition of the simple guitar and some EDM vibes, *indie*.

Maybe that's why he was more popular with a certain crowd of young people over the mainstream, which even explained his popularity abroad in such a short span of time since his foray into the music scene.

"Doesn't he look a little like a younger Jason Mraz?" a teen-aged girl excitedly asked her companion, who replied, "No, he resembles John Mayer somewhat." She differed.

Whichever star he resembled, he was good-looking in his own way. He was handsome, although few would agree about him being an *Adonis*, yet he had this look which would prompt women to describe him as 'mysteriously cute'!

After the musical night and his first concert outside his native country, he was immensely congratulated by everyone backstage.

"Why Lancashire for your foreign debut?" asked a lanky blond guy from the local press.

"Where else would I be? Hey even the Beatles started out here!" he laughed, "Well if it hadn't been for my friend and fellow musician, Russel Davis, I would have never been here. We met during our music days in London, you see, when we collaborated. Plus there's quite a lot of Indians out here, eh!"

Russel Davis was a rising sensation in his country and he more or less pulled the *local* crowd, who were not all disappointed with the amazing singer from India, they liked him immediately!

....

As he was sitting there backstage sipping coffee, some Indian origin fans came up and congratulated him. They wanted to know how things were back in India given the music scene, and he had to update them with all the happenings, although bored and greatly uninterested himself. They thanked him for sparing his time and for his courtesy, complimented him on his music and retreated. But someone called out and commented that they especially loved the lyrics to his songs, 'so unique and different in its simplicity yet with such meaningful undertones, one could but only relate to them'.

"Should I compliment you or is there a songwriter?" the man asked.

Just then something happened the young singer was suddenly caught off-guard by what the individual just said. All throughout the evening everybody had complimented him on his music, but for the first time somebody talked about his lyrics, well they were not *his* lyrics, but at this phase of his career, it was the only thing he cared about the most.

What good was music if there were no lyrics, where was the song? He thought.

He was transfixed for a while, as if hit by a blow. He felt the vacuum, deep and empty. It seemed as if his life was devoid of lyrics and with only the music, the song was incomplete, *their song.* He was in love with his songwriter, but she had left him. And he didn't himself realize he loved her until she was gone. Oh his over-enhancing sense of pride! How he had denied his own feelings, because he was too scared? *'What a fool I was!'*

At this remembrance he was greatly affected, his manner, his demeanor suddenly changed. Blurting out something in reply, he decided to call it a night and return to his hotel room. He was no longer interested in all that was happening around him and all he wanted was to be left alone. He summoned his manager to arrange for it. But his organizers were upset. They were having a party. Even Russel Davis made an early exit. They wanted him to meet up with all the people – the Indians there, but he refused, excused himself and left.

****

It was quite late and everybody had retired to their chambers. Sitting on the chair, the lights dim, in front of her dressing-table mirror, she looked into it and sighed; she had lied to the very person staring at her – her own self depicted by her reflection.

Oh, what a lie she was living! Preparations were in full swing for her big day and she was about to marry her *dream guy* when actually the very *love of her life* was a million miles away from her and didn't even know that she was pining for him.

She never had the chance to tell him that she loved him. The one time she had tried to give vent to her feelings, he had pushed her away and was oh so cold! She could take it no more, his ignorance of her feelings, and the hard wall that he put up, made her leave for good. How she had missed him and how hard it was for her to deny her feelings the time when he came back! But he was no static cling and never wanted the strings of commitment to tie him up. Free love, just love, was it possible?

When it was actually the time to take her own life seriously, or so she thought, she had left *songwriting* and *him* and abandoned *their song.* Now she was getting married, *to someone else.*

What a step! And yet for *everybody's sake!* But didn't she have a voice of her own? *The one that was hidden and could mould any music into a song.* Why was she trying to please everybody when pleasing everybody was a key to failure? Poor girl, she had chosen to live her life on her knees. She felt it was the only thing left to do, no choice. But as the saying goes, "When everything is in ruins, search among the wreckage, there is a golden opportunity hidden in the ruins!" Indeed so.

- *x* -

II

The sun was bright; its strong rays making everything seem golden and fresh. It was a brilliant morning with a clear sky. She was awoken from deep sleep by the sound of repeated knocks on her door. It was her old nurse waiting outside.

The older woman anxiously declared: He had come over and was waiting for her downstairs. He wanted to take her out for some pre-wedding shopping.

Immediately, she jumped out of bed and started to get ready. She hurried with her things. She could not dare disappoint her would-be husband! And thus she was running about her room, worrying about what to wear in order to look *presentable* before people. After all she might bump into some acquaintances or even her in-laws! An open drawer here, some clothes on the bed there, shoes in the closet and make-up & toiletries in the bathroom! Gosh! Thanks to the presence of her old nurse, who helped settle it all!

Well, it seems all her efforts paid off, as her fiancé profoundly exclaimed that she looked *pretty* when she went out into the yard where he was waiting for her, leaning on his car.

Looking at him, she tried to analyze her feelings for him. He was her childhood friend, they had almost grown up together and she really liked him but it was nothing like *love*, no blushing warmth at his sight, no bone-chilling excitement at the sound of his voice, no crazy thoughts, no wavering awkwardness, just plainness; and yet she accepted his proposal and her family's plea for an arranged marriage at such a young age, 22!

As he opened the car door for her, he smiled. She looked at his profile as he went over to settle into the driver's seat, buckling his seat-belt, switching on the ignition. Then they drove-off. She thought how he often told her that he *liked* her but love was a little difficult and she guessed he didn't feel any either. *Here were two people trying to enter into such a sacred*

21

institution, that of marriage, and they hardly felt any love for the other.

Then why are we doing it? Her inner voice clenched, as if in dismayed anger, but she dared not question out loud.

****

It was mid-afternoon and the sun was bright but the temperature was terribly low. Summers in Europe were hardly warm; at least the sun was out. Though they were driving through the city, something was peaceful about it unlike in India were the vehicles never stopped honking and it was always congested with such heavy traffic on the road!

Lancashire was a beautiful place, with the seaside town of Blackpool being a major tourist attraction. The English county's historical aura and the reminiscences of industrial revolution added to its charm. Its mixture of coastal plains and hill-tops with free-flowing rivers added to its unique topography, plus the presence of forests and moors made the place really picturesque.

Interestingly even, the place had a major music scene, not just contemporary but also its share of folks and classical music, no wonder he was drawn to it, even before meeting Russel Davis. He always wanted to visit the place where his icons, the Beatles, first started out, in Liverpool.

They were driving to the airport as he was flying to London that afternoon. He intended on spending an entire week in London, anonymously. He loved the streets, the cold weather and the occasional rain, perfect setting to make some music, like the old days, and he smiled at the thought.

After the usual procedures at the airport, he got his boarding call and headed for his flight. As the plane got ready for take-off, he was excited. He loved the way the aircraft took up speed, as fast as a race car, and glided into the air. Despite the uneven breathing patterns and the hollowness of the stomach, he loved the view from the window, as the world seemed upside down! Below the human settlement looked like model doll houses and the fast moving traffic seemed like toy cars in a make-believe expressway!

After a few minutes as the plane got stable, it became almost boring. The blues seemed to come back, the loneliness bit sharp. He tried to divert his mind of other things, only less successfully. He tried reading but his mind seemed elsewhere. So, he closed his eyes and tried to meditate.

The plane experienced some "clear-weather turbulence". He opened his eyes, straitened up and looked outside the window; suddenly he was overcome by a sense of pleasure as he found himself in the abode of clouds, white in varying shapes, amidst the blue of the sky. It was like another world, a heavenly tinge to it and absolutely stunning, the sun rays making the cottony white clouds sparkle! Lovely, he thought, his mind already humming to a new melody!

-x-

III

The Heathrow airport was crowded as usual; filled with countless passengers moving in and moving out bag-baggage, some weary, a few jubilant, perhaps to be back home, and others reticent. He saw people waiting to receive those who had just arrived and was suddenly reminded of that voice in the beginning of the movie "Love Actually", those words how *love* can be found in the Arrivals gate of the Heathrow airport, and something inside him strung, as he expressionlessly walked, along with his manager, to the exit. They walked to the car waiting for them, and then drove-off to their destination, he was to stay in one of the Hilton hotels.

****

The grandfather clock downstairs struck 12 times; it was 12 AM miles away in India. The lights in the neighborhood houses began to go-off one by one as she sat in her balcony, gazing at the stars, a rare sight in the city though that night was uncommon. Three houses down the lane, the late-night party had just begun.

"Hey, I have this housewarming party at my place tonight, drop in for a few drinks?" said her neighbor in her adenoidal voice.

"Okay, I'll think about it," She said.

"Ok, whatever," her neighbor couldn't care less.

She was un-interested herself, but for politeness sake, thought she would consider it, but after that little conversation, she decided against it.

Now she was sitting there all alone, deep in thought. Maybe she should have gone after all. The emptiness seemed to cut in deep. She could not help thinking about *him*. *Where was he now?* It was days since she had tried to think about his whereabouts and had dared to think about him.

All the suppressed emotions of the past few days occupied her mind completely, sending her spirits in a jitter. Everything seemed to be moving so damn fast, so many things were happening all at once. She was forced to undertake life-changing decisions and she had barged into it all too quick, when all she really wanted was some alone time, to think things over and to deal with it. Suddenly she felt so sad, so terribly sad and heartbroken and angry at herself. Soon her eyes were flooded with tears, as the long drawn flood-gates opened and the tears streamed down her cheeks. She cried silently, strung by a deep pain inside. She felt so torn and weary as if *happiness* had been sucked out of her life by some secret, unseen *dementor*.   Not even the metaphor of dementor[1] made her smile.

She thought. *Why am I doing it? Why? I can't do it. I can't take it anymore.*

But she had done it anyway; agreeing to get married at such a young age, abandoning her talent,

---

[1] J.K.Rowling, "Harry Potter Series", Bloomsbury Publishing (UK).

her love for songwriting, her career, and leaving behind her friends and the one she loved because she wanted *stability*? *What?* All her life, she had always taken the safe side, ditched risks, and listened to what others had to say. *Had she ever listened to her own heart? Done the things she really wanted to do?* She needed to take a stand, to be brave and to make something of her life. She had tried to, when she had met him and they became a team, making songs, doing what they loved but....she had run away at the first sight of complexity!

Maybe it's too late now....

And the night lingered, too long until dawn.

-   x   -

IV

London very well kept his privacy; he was not less a commoner there. He was least likely to be recognized on the street, perhaps even brushed off as a mere tourist. Walking along the pavement all alone, he rejoiced at the idea; it reminded him of his old days when he was just a student at the University of London and often the city streets had been his only respite when he wanted a break from the hostel life on weekends. While he had loved to lose himself in the romance of the city, i.e. London with its iconic ambience, *red, white and gray;* it was while spending time with his two friends, Tim and Roger, that he had seen and learnt a lot about the street music scene there, and it was a completely new experience for him. He immensely loved the energy which was to influence a couple of his songs later.

It had been days since he had felt so free. It was impossible to move around like that in India, especially in his home city. Even a busy metropolis like Mumbai did not spare him. Someone or the other would recognize him at the social events that he so rarely attended.

Walking about, with his spirits in a flutter, he came to a halt all of a sudden in front of a large shop window. *A familiar spot.*

He stood there intently gazing at the object on the other side of the glass. It was a music shop displaying a guitar on sale. He was a musician, had a great collection of all possible kinds of guitars, and this was just another one such, but it was not ordinary. It held a position of importance for him at this moment, like it had done for someone else almost a year ago. It was the same guitar that had captured her attention and she was struck by the brand new display in the shop window. They used to pass by that street often, and always checked out that certain shop.

"Eeshaan, look at this one!" she had said excitedly, "Doesn't it seem pretty amazing?"

"Hey, we don't have time for that." He did not even look.

"But you'll love it, maybe it's an antique." She was so sure.

"Not antique. Come on, this shop doesn't deal in that kind of stuff."

"But..."

"Lyla, we're getting late." He was almost irritated. "Man, it's just a guitar, no big deal!" said his expression as he walked off, leaving her behind.

"Okay, alright."

He had failed to understand her enthusiasm then, and did not even give her the opportunity to pursue the same. But now he did. *Maybe it's too late, but not too late to preserve some memories.*

Thoughtfully he entered the shop, bought the guitar and ordered it to be delivered to his hotel room.

"Good choice, Sir," said the shop lady, "Now this piece was an antique and ironically nobody realized it over the past one year since it was on display."

He was caught by surprise at this, and he couldn't help smiling as he walked out the door. He resumed his solitary walk but with a difference. Suddenly he was so happy, that for the first time in days, he actually felt good. He beamed from ear to ear as he thought about it. *Now that was something!*

- x -

V

She sat surrounded by gorgeous wedding apparel and magnificent jewelry, her grandmother's, so old yet so precious, it's worth further raised by its longevity, while her relatives praised its grandeur. A dream wedding indeed, everything that any girl could ever desire! She was *perfectly* happy, she assured herself.

"Oh my god, Lyla, you are getting married in a palace like royalty!" exclaimed her friend.

"It's a hotel, not a real palace," said their always accurately correct other friend in her matter of fact voice.

"Yeah whatever," but the former was starry-eyed, "still, isn't it something?!"

"Yes, indeed. You can't imagine how envious I am!" teased the bride's cousin, barging in. And they all burst into giggles.

All their relatives couldn't stop praising both the arrangements and the bride, and she only smiled at them in reply. Indeed she was having a fairytale wedding, the big day that every girl dreamt of, and probably the happiest, but *only if she was really happy.*

She smiled again before taking leave of her relatives, friends and acquaintances all of whom that had come visiting, leaving them to indulge in further admiration of the arrangements and everything thus associated. She rushed upstairs to her room. She was getting married in two days, but today there was a task to accomplish.

Once inside, she took out her phone and without wasting any more time, thinking or otherwise, made a long distance ISD call. She waited breathlessly, hearing the long rings till someone received it at the other end.

The voice was unrecognizable. Had she dialed a wrong number?

"Hello... Hello? Yes?" said a stranger's voice.

She took a deep breath and spoke all at once, "Hello...Is this Eeshaan's number? If not, I'm sorry, it just..."

"Yes, yes, this is his number. I'm actually his manager," the voice on the other side interrupted her in mid-sentence, and said reassuringly, "I know you must be one of his close friends since you have this number, but he rarely takes even his personal calls these days."

"Okay," she didn't know what to say, but somehow managed, "May I ...May I have a word with him?"

"Oh, I'm really sorry but he is out and I'm afraid will be so for some time. But if you have any messages, I shall convey..."

"No, no messages," saying, she cut-off.

She did not want to think about it. All of it left her overwhelmed.

....

After that call, her entire day was marked by a sense of low, a downward spiral despite the accustomed loneliness that had come to mark her present stance. *Maybe his voice would have been her undoing.* She tried to hide her feelings; tried hard to be happy, but in vain. Something inside kept nagging her. *"You should tell him. He should know."* But she could not gather the strength for a second attempt. *No, how could she,* she thought. But she needed to do something! She couldn't go about like this! Couldn't let it just be!

So, to keep her thoughts at bay, she made an

attempt to keep herself busy. All her family members, friends and close relatives had gathered. They were to have a close-knit party together to celebrate the occasion.

They all sat there on the lawn, her friends and cousins, chatty and excited. The food was scrumptious, so were the drinks. But despite the happy mayhem somehow she seemed lost in the midst of it all. Her immediate company remarked on it but she shrugged it off. Pre-wedding jitters, they assumed.

"Hey, you know this band, they are called 'the Grouplove', I mean they are pretty good," said her friend Tanaya so as to change the subject and indulge in something that she liked. They had been in college together, and back then had shared a passion for good music.

"Never heard of them, what sort of music do they make?" asked Lyla's cousin instead, as if sensing the situation.

"They are this Indie rock band from the States. I mean, I mainly like their lyrics, you know they have those lyrics that are different yet you can so well understand them," She replied and directly addressing the bride said, "Lyla, you are a lyricist yourself, you should definitely check them out..."

"I'm no longer one; I've left all of it now." She cut her midway.

"But, why? It was your career! I mean even before that, remember how you used to keep scribbling all those lines just everywhere! You were crazy and you just loved it!"

"Yeah, that was in the past, when I was younger and careless and did not realize the value of things." Getting up as if to leave, she added, "You know, life's too precious to waste it pursuing your unfulfilled dreams."

"But..." before her friend could complete her sentence, and before she could leave, her old grand-uncle spoke from behind, "I completely disagree with you, dear. Life is too precious to waste it not living your dreams. If you don't listen to your heart you can never be happy."

Something clicked inside her; could her grand-uncle guess her feelings? She could stop no longer. She took leave of them all and sped off to her room.

Taking out her laptop, she began composing a mail, *to him*. She wrote everything that was in her mind, that she was getting married and that she didn't hate him anymore and in fact, a little reluctantly added that she actually *loved* him. But it seemed that luck was not on her side! There was some internet connection failure and the screen showed 'sending failed'.

She almost lost her temper and banged her fist on the table. Now after this, a third attempt was completely out of the question!

That night, sleep seemed like a distant entity. As she lay awake in bed, somehow her thoughts were drawn back to the time she had spent pursuing her dreams, wild and passionate, even ready to fly! Those times seemed a bit too unrealistic now, even funny. But back then she was so sure of things, breaking out of her shell, daring, taking risks, for all she had wanted was there right in front of her. *But was it really?*

-   x   -

VI

It was the perfect weather; sunny but not too hot. There was a slight breeze which kept things neat and the sky was the bluest of blue, with white clouds that seemed to take on any shape you could imagine! Most of all, there was celebration in the air in the large country house down the road, as the wedding preparations of their *little* daughter were in full swing! There were sounds of people's chatter and laughter and everybody seemed to be in such a merry mood!

Now, one can only really imagine an Indian wedding, if one has actually attended it. The big fat Indian Wedding, with its plethora of countless rituals, ceremonies and customs and all the traditions, *a predominance of colours;* the merry-making, all the music from folk to rock and even an aura of classical (!), the bottles of booze and the food, some even boasting of a worldwide cuisine; and most of all the joy of a get-together of family members, friends and relatives, kept alive by crazy jokes and some essential drama!

Everybody seemed so busy that morning,

engaging in some stuff or otherwise! Decorations - the flowers here, the chandelier there, the lights, the music. Kids playing their naughty little games, running about! Flowers in baskets; food being prepared; guests arriving; gifts and greetings; new acquaintances; so much was happening all at once!

The young women of the house and their friends were in their best attire, trying to outshine one another. *Does this colour look good on me? Oh I can't find my matching earrings! Wow, I love this dress!* And the young men, equally charming, trying to impress the ladies, hoping to find their own match!

The young, the old and those in the middle, all equally elated; and a traditional Indian wedding in the making!

Amidst all these, the Bride sat all alone in her room upstairs, dressed in finery. The silver of her attire highlighted her light skin tone, minimal make-up kept *au naturel* and with heavily Kohled eyes and bright red lips, she indeed looked stunning. Her soft black hair was tied in a bun with grand little hair accessories that gave it a neatly-tousled look.

She just sat there, her hands dyed with '*mehendi*', adorned with jewels, bangles clinking on her wrists, waiting; waiting for that moment which she secretly dreaded, when things would no longer be the same again. *Was it really worth it?* She had resolved to carry this heavy burden, for the sake of things, but how long would she be able to carry it?

And then, the phone rang... a call which was to change her life forever, but it was only later did she realize how important this phone-call indeed was!

Its Eeshaan, was her immediate reaction, and her breath quickened as she reached for it. But she was in for a disappointment and her feelings altered, sank a little, when she saw her fiancé's name flash onscreen.

"Hi! I, um…there's something I need you to know." was his first response when she answered the phone and said "Hello." He sounded sort of excited, *so unlike him,* she thought.

"Now? What is it?" She was a bit startled.

"Yes. Actually it's urgent..I, uh.." after a short pause, as if he was making an inward decision, he said, "Okay, meet me at the airport, now!"

"What? Wha..what are you saying? Airport? Now?!" this time she was really startled.

"Yes. I'm sorry, I'll explain later. My flight's in an hour. And please, please don't tell anybody. Only you, please, I beg of you." He was literally pleading.

"Okay, okay, okay!" she didn't know what she was saying, she was so surprised and almost shouted, "What about the wedding?!"

"Look, I don't have much time. I'll explain later. Everything will be alright," and getting no reply from the other end, said, "I promise.. Just come and please hurry!" Then he hung up.

She was transfixed for a while, she couldn't believe the turn of events. *What the heck was happening?!* But she couldn't just wait, she needed to know.

- x -

VII

Grabbing her car keys, she rushed out of her room, running down the stairs, not giving a second look to the others around her. She walked out the door into the lawns and half ran, half walked to the garage, in her heavy wedding attire.

A new chauffer had been hired for a couple of days for the wedding, and he almost stood up, surprised at seeing the bride and asked, "Madam, do you want anything?"

"Yes, get me my car, please. Here are the keys." She said, handing him the same.

He nodded and went in, but when he drove out of the garage, he looked out the driving seat window and said, "Do you want me to drive you, madam?"

She had wanted to refuse right-away, but answered in the affirmative when she thought of the long drive to the airport in the heavy traffic at this hour, and that too in her bridal attire which was not even easy to walk in. She got into the car, telling him the destination.

Meanwhile, her cousin, who had seen her rushing outside and then getting into the car, ran to her to find out what was the matter, but before she could call out or signal them to stop, they had already driven off. Her cousin wasted no time in informing the family about the sudden, unexplained departure of the bride. Everyone was left in confusion and anxiety, and all activities came to a halt. Repeated calls to her cell-phone were of no avail as she had left it in her room amidst the rush. But it was her old Grand Uncle in charge of the household matters who decided to keep an open mindset and waited for her return, giving her the much needed space.

The young Chauffer was quite an expert, and in no time was able to reach the airport, driving through short-cuts, lanes and gullies, whizzing past the traffic! As they reached their destination, she thanked the young man and rushed to the main enclosure.

Her fiancé was waiting outside with a ticket for her and thus they were able to enter the general waiting area without further delay. It was about 11.00 in the morning and the area was crowded. Despite the rush, many people looked in awe at the bride, thanks to her attire; but she was in no mood for it. As he led her to one of the seats, she faced him and demanded an immediate explanation. He told her to calm down and sit, which she refused and said instead,

"What did you want to tell me that you had to call me all the way out here knowing quite well that it would create such a scene in public?!" She was so angry at him for all the rush that she didn't realize that she had raised her voice.

"Okay, please calm down, will you? I'm sorry, I really am but this is important," he said and added, "Please hear me out, will you please? I know this is hard for both of us but it needs to be done."

"So you are running away because you don't want us to get married? Why create so much drama? You could have told me earlier, saved us both time and money, could've.."

"Hey, It's nothing like that and it's not about you, okay."

"Then what is it? You were my childhood friend; I thought we had no secrets!"

"Really? We were that close? We hardly know each other! And we were about to get married! Do you realize that?"

"Then why did you propose?"

"I..I..I don't know, I didn't know what I was doing! I'm.." He seemed lost for words.

"Hey, hey, let's not really create a scene. Why are we fighting? We'll not get married, it's done, ok!" She said. Surprisingly she found herself liking the turn of events.

"Yeah. I'm sorry but..uh..there's more." He said and continued, "I really like you. In fact, you are the only girl I have really liked so much, and maybe in an alternate universe I would've married you for real."

She was startled, *what was he saying*?

"Wait let me finish…. But I don't *love* you, and I cannot love any girl ever 'cause there's only one man that I really love and right now I need to be with him, and I'm sorry but I can't do this *straight guy* thing anymore 'cause I'm not straight."

She just looked at him, her eyes wide, and he said, "Yes, I'm gay and maybe all these years I was a coward, but I'm not anymore. I know I tried the extreme step, for my family's sake, for everybody's sake, but no more. It's my life after all and I can't afford to lose myself in the process, not to speak of ruining your life too."

She was too surprised to speak but the things that he said struck her deep; it was the same case with her too. She too was going ahead with her wedding for *everybody's sake, if only she could have been that brave!*

He continued, "I had been contemplating running away these past few days and I was scared, but something happened this morning and here I am!" He shrugged, "Actually I had decided to leave without telling anybody but then I realized that I owed you an explanation, so this is it, and I'm so sorry..." He held her hand, and as a sudden gesture of what was, *we are on the same boat brother (?!),* she went in and gave him a hug.

"So you are alright, huh?" he asked.

"Yes." She was laughing.

"Hey, you need to fall in love, take your time, you know." He said.

But she didn't want to think about it now, so she changed the subject, "Where are you headed now?"

"Los Angeles. Our country still thinks our love is a crime, pity. Anyway, I don't care. What is freedom if we don't have any? Better be someplace where we can live with dignity."

"What about your family?" she was concerned.

"What about them? They will make some noise now but eventually accept it. My parents know about me, it's just that they are scared of the society, and maybe they needed this, so that they can broaden their outlook." He said, a bit broken inside.

Just then the final announcement for his flight's security check was made. They shook hands and bade farewell, and then Arav left. As he walked away, she looked at him, the Arav she had known to be so quiet and resilient had dared to take a step, no matter how drastic but something that needed to be done, and she thought, *shouldn't I be doing the same?*

- x -

VIII

On the drive back home, she was lost in thought. She unconsciously looked out the car window at the life in motion outside; everybody was in such a rush, it seemed, *chasing concrete dreams in the city streets*, but for her, time seemed to take a slow and easy pace, after these past days of rush and tension.

She reflected on the state of events that day; she didn't feel bad at all but was rather happy and a bit envious of her friend's courage. She even felt relieved as if a heavy burden had fallen off her shoulders. She was amused at the sudden happenings. It was strange for someone like Arav. She had never suspected it, let alone expected it, but it was again evident how little they knew of each other. After all, whatever happens does happen for good.

....

Later that evening, they all sat in the living room after the guests had left, a few friends and some relatives, family members and the former bride herself, everybody engaged in some great discussion. There were loud voices and a few sobs, some empty low tones and even occasional mumblings. There was confusion in the air, but she sat aloof, without speaking to anybody, reflecting, smiling inwardly, she felt she had learnt a lesson and that it had really been necessary. *Man, she needed that!*

It was her life after all. She need not abide by the so –called rules of conduct that every woman/ man was expected to follow. 'Society asks of you to do this or that, otherwise you have lost it' was utter nonsense. Her former fiancé too was a victim; at least he had dared to break free! She needed to do so too! Why was she punishing herself? Where was her voice? That same little voice that had shaped melodies, to turn them into songs of change?

....

For the first time in days Lyla felt free and light. She was introspective, yet still feeling as if something was incomplete, as if a chapter of her life was half-written, ink splattered on its pages, no effort for a conclusion. Again, none but she needed to strive for her own destiny. She needed to re-embark on her passion and give *love* a chance...

Eeshaan had all he wanted, a career in music, an international appeal in the making, a job that he was passionate about, fame, recognition and the lingering taste of sweet success but he still had a 'blank space' left. *Love* was all he needed to feel complete but was it possible without *her*?

....

It was almost midnight but the city was wide awake, the lights and sounds piercing the cold London air. He stood there, holding on to the railings by the river, watching the Thames gush by in the moonlight. Soon, it began to drizzle and some of the people nearby walked away, while a few opened their umbrellas, but he just remained there, feeling the rain on his skin, enjoying it all, *little moments that make up life*.

-   x   -

The laid back musings of autumn was only a reminder of where the story of Lyla and Eeshaan stood in the backdrop of falling leaves, brown and red, and a chill in the air. Their story had unfolded in the brightness of summer embedded in warmth. Two different individuals with a passion each of their own, each different in their endeavors yet tied by the same strings of music, one unsure the other in pursuit of a sure path, stumbled upon one other, to realize their destinies and in the process find love... Only *Fate* had other designs.

-   x   -

SUMMER

IX

A few years earlier...

March is that month of the year when most parts of India is blessed with spring. The weather is generally pleasant, the sun is not too sharp and the sky, mostly clear with a tinge of blue, adorned with soft cottony white clouds. Everywhere around flowers of different hues is in full bloom and the trees equally green and elated like the grasses below. Quite an appealing sight and no one does it better than Delhi!

In such a beautiful lazy Saturday afternoon in spring, she found herself wondering, *"What am I doing here?"*

The location in consideration was Connaught Place, a picturesque urban area in the heart of New

Delhi, with reminiscences of Colonial era architecture, mostly built along the lines of the European Renaissance styled in Classical essence; a place where a young enthusiast will never get bored thanks to its range of interest from plain shopping and all sorts of worldly cuisines to activities like theatres and musicals.

"Come on Lyla, let's hurry!" her cousin said pulling her arm, "Or else we'll get late and it would be real embarrassing to barge in like that in the middle of the show!"

"Yeah okay," she said, falling behind her fast-paced companion.

Both cousins were headed to the venue of a stage-play.

....

"Wasn't it good? It was so good! I have never seen a better play. The acting was so natural and the storyline..." Her cousin's words seemed to go above her head, she was the least interested; yes the play was good and that was it.

They were standing next to the exit of the theatre auditorium, waiting for a friend who would be joining them shortly.

"Yeah it was," said she, unable to hide her disinterest.

"Not into it, are you?" asked her companion.

"Well, sort of, you know, perhaps it's not my thing," she sighed.

"Okay, so what is your *thing* then?" her cousin

44

asked.

"I don't know, you know, I haven't figured it out yet!" she said.

At this her cousin gave a matter of fact look and said, "Anyway rest apart, did you have a good time today?"

She gave her cousin an apologizing smile and said, "Frankly, I lost track of the play midway but no doubt it was good, only it couldn't hold me till the end" and shrugging her shoulders added, "And I liked the background score, it really did add to the essence of the play, capturing the right angles." She was talking more to herself now, almost brooding and her cousin commented, "Was there even a background score?!"

"Duh, of course there was!" She said.

"Whatever, it's like you dwell in a different world altogether!" her cousin was smirking.

Before she could reply, someone from the back addressed them suddenly, "Hey, are you guys talking about the background score?"

It was a rather good-looking young man with a beard yet more bohemian in his dressing sense than looks. "I'm sorry I was standing out here for a while and couldn't help eavesdropping since I heard you talking about the play."

They were a little startled but her cousin said instead, "Oh yes, and yes. Actually my cousin here, I mean, she was so totally talking about it."

At this the man glanced at Lyla and she blurted out, "Yeah, it was quite...Rather good." She was suddenly caught off-guard by her cousin's address, *damn Maya!*

"Thanks! I mean actually..." Before the man could finish, Lyla's cousin, Maya, interrupted, "Was it you? Were you responsible for the music?"

"Oh no, no, it was my friend. I mean, he's not here right now. He's this budding musician. He's generally into indie stuff, and it was his first brush with something like this. I'll tell him people did appreciate." He clarified.

Lyla found herself looking intently at the guy when he spoke about his friend and before she could even think, she spoke all of a sudden, "This musician friend of yours, I mean, is he not into this stuff? He did a really good job."

"Yes, he's actually quite talented but he's still trying to find his big break. You see, back in college he was quite a star but now it's the real world and it's not so easy but he's so intent on certain things!" she was quite intrigued by this unknown man about whom his friend was really concerned and the friend went on to say, "So, I persuaded him to give a shot at this, it's actually my play, you see."

"Oh really, this was your play? I should say it was really good, in fact, great, you know..."

And her cousin and the playwright got talking. They were the few people left out there and all the while as she found herself slipping off from their conversation, whilst she couldn't help wondering about the musician guy!

- x -

X

Two weeks had passed by since then but the sweet aura of spring was still in the air. It was another working day and the sun was out and the roads abuzz with never-ending traffic, honking cars and the sound of engines; but amidst the concrete mayhem, bloomed flowers, somewhat pale yet pretty, thanks to the efforts of social forestry in the city. No wonder New Delhi was the greenest city in the country, if not the cleanest, and there was at least some amount of soothing green to deal with the day-to-day madness!

"Mid-semester break starts this Saturday! I'm so excited!" said her over-enthusiastic friend as they walked along the interesting streets of the charming North Campus of the University of Delhi, "So, what are you gonna do?"

"I don't know. It tends to get boring at home and I haven't planned on anything. At least you are going to Ladakh!" Lyla sighed.

"I know right, I'm so looking forward to it, we've been planning this trip for ages and finally we are doing it! Hey, if only you could come," said the friend.

"No. You know, I'm not much of a traveler and then again..." She didn't know what to say, it always seemed so difficult to break out of her comfort zone.

But before she could finish, her friend's phone started to ring and she excused herself. She could hear her friend speaking excitedly about the trip to someone, perhaps her boyfriend from Hindu college. *She was so cool.*

****

Later that day,
He was reclining on the arm-chair in his friend's airy living room.

"Dude, it's not happening! It's like I'm running out of ideas. I did try, I did venture into other genres yet somehow I feel it's not enough, there's got to be something more."

"Come on Man, now those girls did like your work!" another friend smirked at him.

He rolled his eyes and threw the cushion at the speaker who was trying hard to play chords on the guitar. He shouted, "Hey!", and giving up on the task at hand said, "God, a C minor's not easy!"

"If only you really did know anything about guitars!" Eeshaan said, at which his friend replied, "That's because *you* taught me; you really suck as a teacher!"

"Alright, you guys," interrupted the playwright friend, "Eeshaan, what is it, man?"

"I just don't know. It's like I'm this actor who's forgotten how to act! It feels like I'm going nowhere and all that about 'true calling' and stuff; now it feels like crap!"

"Look, I understand. I've been there. You are just passing through a low phase in your career; take it easy, man, give yourself a break or something," said the playwright.

"Career? Did I ever even start one?!" he was almost frustrated; and looking at his two best-friends said, "You guys are the lucky ones who're actually doing something real. Jeff's got his chef's job, you are creating plays but as for me, I'm still stuck at figuring out the right stuff!"

And before his friends could reply he said, "Look guys, you are my best pals and I know you understand, but it's little hard for me, okay."

"Yeah, but it's hardly lucky when you are stuck under somebody with a set of guidelines, and no longer have the freedom to experiment with your favourite cuisines! Where is the passion, I ask?" Jeff said and further added, "It ain't fun working under somebody who dictates you the rules of the game!"

"You've got a point, buddy" said a voice from the doorway as another friend walked in, "What about starting your own place?"

"Hey!" everybody greeted him in unison, "Back from work so soon? Didn't know Cairo was so near!" joked Jeff.

"You bet!" said Arden. He was the most successful of the lot, having bagged a job with a travel magazine that sponsored his travels all over Asia and Africa as part of a promotion for tourism in the two continents plagued by socio-political problems.

"Well, my job is to find the gold underneath the dirt and whom do I need to succor today?" Arden said.

Everyone looked at Eeshaan.

Arden went up to him and hugged him hard and said patting him on the back, "Hey man, take it easy!

Now that I'm back, the weekend's not gonna be lousy! And there'll be music!"

- x -

XI

It was the usual Friday morning lectures, one day to go and a much-needed reprieve for the week. The girl in the next row couldn't help yawning and it was just the first period!

While on her drive to college she noticed how with winter almost over and spring lighting up days and nights with its natural exuberance, there was this feeling of bliss in the air, something romantic, a sweetened sugar-coated tinge to existence, with all the flowers and the sunshine and the bright blue sky, the flirty breeze tingling one's senses. All of it made her feel so poetically heightened. *I could write a love song!* Well, love was by all means the flavor of the season!

Later tucked inside her classroom in Miranda House, she was mechanically scribbling down parts of what the teacher spoke, but couldn't help let her mind wander and momentarily suffered an imaginative blackout! Oh how exhilarating it felt to imagine that she was instead on a train, travelling across Europe, passing by postcard pretty locations, enjoying her solitude. Just then a handsome stranger approached her asking if she had ever witnessed

Venice at night? But before she could even talk to him, the bell rang, cruelly waking her up from her daydream! Humph, back to reality!

Later during the last period of the day as the professor kept dictating key points to remember, she was distracted and more so disillusioned with routine. Instead, turning around she found her friend surfing the net, looking up – Ladakh. So she spoke in the lowest of whispers and said, "Do you know how I envy you? Guess I need to look for something to rescue me from this rut!"

"Yeah you should, definitely should...Something constructive?" the other girl asked.

"Dunno, let's see. I'm sorta clueless." She replied.

The day ended with a load of assignments and looming tests on the horizon, but no worries- they'd all be done only at the last minute!

Miranda House, the college that she studied in, was an enigma in red brick, it's ambience a perfect blend of nature and heritage, and each time Lyla walked in through the gate, it made her feel like she was tracing and making history, thereof.

****

The sun was out, shiny and bright and the trees swayed in the pleasant breeze. As they walked around the shady green North Campus of Delhi University, they were reminded of their graduation days there. With Arden in town, both of them were just visiting the place in an attempt to revive the same old days when they had met and had become friends. Bunking lectures and running off to CP or sitting on the Arts faculty lawns at night, Eeshaan with his guitar, the D-school canteen round ups and the countless Xeroxes at Patel Chest before exams, enjoying a game or two of football at the University Stadium, attending the festivals in different colleges, and trying to socialize with Miranda House girls whenever the opportunity presented itself! Those glory days of theirs!

....

They were walking on the sidewalk, chatting, when all of a sudden, a Royal Enfield Bullet slowed down nearby. Somebody called out Eeshaan's name. It was a guy in a bike, unfamiliar. Eeshaan responded thinking it was an old classmate or acquaintance. The guy stopped his motorcycle and while still sitting there, held out his hand as if to shake it and said, "Eeshaan right? You used to study here in St Stephens?"

"Yes," Eeshaan said, "I'm sorry but I am unable to recognize you."

"I'm afraid, you don't know me, it's just the other way round," the guy chuckled, "I was in the same college and I remember seeing you perform several times in the college fests. You were really good."

"Thanks man," Eeshaan smiled back.

"Yeah, so what are you doing these days? Probably signed up by some big records company I bet", he said.

"Well, not exactly," laughed Eeshaan, "What about you?"

"Me, I decided to listen to that nagging voice inside, for a change," laughed the guy, "and I am now a professional deep sea diver."

"Whoa," it was Arden who spoke this time, "that's really cool. Wait, what did you say your name was?"

"Raj Johar", he said.

"Yes, I remember now," said Arden, "The TravelMag did a cover story on you right?"

"Yeah, they did" Raj said, smiling.

"Arden," he said introducing himself and they shook hands, "I work as a travel writer".

"Hey, it was really nice to see you after so long, Eeshaan, Arden, but I have got to go now," saying he started his bullet, "hope to hear your music soon, Eeshaan, I always thought you were real good, man," saying he drove away.

"I think, this was your motivation, man," Arden said to Eeshaan.

"It totally was," said Eeshaan, reflecting upon this small encounter.

-   x -

XII

The morning was pleasant despite the bright sun, with a breath of fresh air and a sense of purity that's only there when the day begins. Since it was a little early, the traffic was lighter. She was in a jubilant mood, more lively than the usual; her eyes shining with excitement and cheeks flushed, as she crossed the street when the lights turned red. Strolling a few blocks down the footpath, she was finally at her destination. Just round the corner of the street, sandwiched between a glossy flower-shop and a showroom of MRF Tyres, was a small Antique shop. Although not an immediate eye-catcher, the little place was quaint when observed carefully, with its glass windows and the little glass door that had a wind-chime which jingled when the door was opened or closed. Inside the décor was light and creamy with a hint of wood and a tinge of peach, such that the items on display were the highlights and stood out.

Though an Antique shop in name and nature, it also *hid* some quirky items which grabbed her attention on her very first visit accompanying her aunt who was an antique lover and collector. The place had an aura of mystery attached to it, that was only evident once one's engrossed, otherwise fooled by its *sweet plain* camouflage and she had liked it instantly!

While browsing around, she had overheard a conversation between the manager of the shop, probably the owner, and somebody on the phone that they were in need of someone, *someone really capable, not just anyone (!),* to manage the shop for a week while she was away on some serious business. She had met several people for the purpose but somehow she was unable to trust any of them. Later, when she had found her aunt in conversation with the lady herself, she too had joined in; and surprisingly for an otherwise shy person, she had gathered the courage to ask the lady directly if she was really in need of a temporary manager, at the same time adding that *she* would love to do it, if the lady thought her fit for the job. At this the shop manager had responded saying,

"Yes, I am in need of someone worthy but" and giving the girl a speculative look said, "What are your qualifications?"

"I am a student" she replied simply, adding, "Oh, and I'll be having my mid-semester break next week and I really need something to do. If you hire me, I promise, I'll..."

"Wait", the lady interrupted her in mid-sentence, eyeing her closely, and then addressing her aunt instead said, "What do you think, madam?"

Her aunt replied with a smile, "Well, I think she would do great" and winked at Lyla.

"Okay, be here next Monday, 8 AM, sharp" the shop owner said in her flat voice.

"Thanks! For sure!" she said excitedly.

"And I don't like it when people are late" the lady said and walked away to the counter to receiver a newcomer.

"No worries. I'll be there!" she was smiling and her aunt whispered into her ear, "Such a cranky pants, your boss there!" and they had both laughed as they walked out the door.

At exactly five minutes to eight that Monday, she reached her destination, the Antique shop.

....

The shop owner, after explaining all the required necessities and allotting her the responsibilities, left for her own destination. But before leaving, she told the girl, "Call me if there's any problem, or if something goes wrong. My phone numbers, e-mail id, everything is on the card here."

"Okay, sure" she already felt like a responsible adult.

"So wish you luck, okay, Bye" For once she was un-business-like.

"Thanks! And happy journey!" she shouted as the older woman opened the door to leave. She waved back from the door and said, "Thanks! See you soon."

Now it was all up to her! Gosh!

Left alone at last, with another young woman, the shop assistant who would join her later, she was excited and nervous at the same time. Strangely happy to indulge in something ordinary yet so different from the usual! Smiling inwardly which was also so clearly visible outside, she began her exploration of the store eager to discover whatever hidden mystery it upheld. It was *hers* for four days, *four days!* That's really a lot of time and what if she discovered something, what if she found *someone!* What if, she became part of something extraordinary, something unique!

While she was lost in her high strung unrealistic thoughts, caught up in her wayward imagination, she did not hear the door clinging, did not notice the figure entering, walking with soft, almost silent footsteps right up to where she was standing, her back to the door. Sensing something perhaps, she turned almost abruptly, her heart pounding/racing, and found herself face to face with a rather peculiar looking lady, probably in her fifties, her heavy make-up failing to hide her age, with a nose that resembled a snout and with a frown etched on her face!

"Ahem", the lady cleared her throat, while the girl stood still trying to recover from the sudden rather unusual, unwanted surprise, and said in her shrill voice, "I need the manager." looking around as if to find her.

"Yes. Um...I'm the manager, well at least for now", she blurted out and composing herself regardless of the stern stare that the woman was giving her, said, "How may I help you?"

"You are the..? Okay, never mind", the woman said almost rolling her eyes, "Show me some antique jewelry, whatever collection you've got."

Not being well-acquainted with that kind of stuff, she was suddenly nervous, freaking out inwards; but before she could get all panicky, the shop-assistant walked in and she breathed a sigh of relief! For the next few hours they tried hard to entertain or rather serve the lady, and by the time she left, it was almost lunchtime and they were famished, given their hard labor!

Most of the afternoon was spent attending to phone-calls and emails from customers enquiring about their orders, and one call from the owner herself, checking to see whether things were running smoothly, though there were no more customers coming in. Soon it was evening and time to close up shop.

As she walked back home, she realized how she had romanticized the whole thing and the reality was far from it, even a little annoying and she sighed, three more days! Phew. Long day, huh?

- x -

XIII

He was exhausted, irritated even, but it was still only 11 o' clock and the real party was yet to begin. The setting was an amalgamation of darkness and light, artificial in its essence, with lights, bright and varied, in sync with the music. The star DJ would only be coming in late for the big game and as of now it was just the jukebox playing. There was dancing and there were drinks too and a hell lot of people, all in their flashy attire, sexiness being the defining element. Amidst all the make-believe fantasy and the fake ecstasy, he somehow felt disillusioned. He could not believe that working in one of the city's best night clubs could be so tiring! *Damn, what a night!*

He was always fascinated by the EDM-dubstep scene in music and had thus decided to give it a go. A few phone calls to the right places and he had landed an opportunity to assist a really high-flying (big-shot) Disc Jockey, Brian Daryl from the States.

He was pretty excited, no wonder! He had come with a lot of expectations of getting a chance to explore electronic dance music from a close angle, only to be disappointed. Turned out, all that he was supposed to do was look into the arrangements regarding the set-up, and do some prior sound-testing and run errands!

The DJ was going to perform in town for three nights in a row at three of the most hip locations and this was the very first night but he was already losing interest. Two more nights still to go and he wanted to give up and leave! But he resolved to hold on to patience; maybe he might learn a thing or two.

....

The phone's display clock showed a quarter to 12. He couldn't wait to get out of there. With all the running around, doing mundane chores and managing all sorts of technical arrangements, the evening had seemed very long and he felt drained and exhausted. Looking around, as if for a means of escape, he caught the eye of a young man, another assistant to the DJ, who seemed to share his disappointment and returned the same hollow expression with a faint smile.

As for the place, there were deep shades of red and blue, in the form of light rays against the otherwise dark setting. The music was scintillating and drinks kept pouring in. Sitting down on one of the bar stools in the corner, sipping his martini, he looked aimlessly around. The guests were busy mingling; voices almost drowned out by the loud music, and everybody was dressed to kill. All were engulfed in the make-believe fantasy night life trying to drown out the day's material sorrows. *They only knew half the truth, not the real picture.* And he let out a little laugh inward, as though he found the whole episode nothing but a stint of mockery.

Lost in deconstructing life truths, he didn't even notice the mysterious figure that came and sat next to him, ever so silently. As if by instinct he turned around; suddenly startled at her proximity, the closeness was alluring. *Or was it the alcohol in his blood stream?* He couldn't quite see her face properly as it was in shadow, only noticed how her hair fell artistically on her shoulders. Then, as if reading his thoughts, she moved to let the light fall on her face.

She was undeniably attractive, with sharp features. But there was something about her eyes which seemed like deep emotional pools. *There was so much in them.*

"The night has failed to hold you, it seems." She spoke suddenly.

"Pardon?" He said, surprised.

Getting no reply from her, he added, "Yeah, disillusionment, that's what I would say."

"So, you are one of the new boys?" She asked and let out a small laugh.

"Only for tonight." He said, "What is so funny?"

"You are telling me that you don't enjoy my man's music right in my face!" She said.

Her man? Was she Brian's girlfriend? "I'm sorry if I have offended you. But I see no reason to apologize. I never meant the music; what I meant was about the background mechanisms."

"Reality is a bitch. Creativity is the easiest thing. Only the tricksters in hideous hats manage to fool the world that it's the other way round", saying, she turned to leave.

"Hey, wait" he called after her, "What about authenticity and genuineness and passion?"

"What about them?" said a deep male voice from the shadows, "They are there, no doubt, within you and visible only to the true beholder." It was Brian Daryl himself, the man of the night.

"As for the rest, its mere commercial crap," she added and Brain came in and held her. "Oh yes, baby, only if they had the slightest idea" he said before sharing a passionate kiss with his lady.

Eeshaan was suddenly overwhelmed by the events. He was slightly enamored by both of them.

"I see you have met Matilda", Brian said addressing Eeshaan.

"In fact, it's the other way round", said Matilda instead and added, "He seemed a lost man amidst the throng of nobodies. But I have never seen so much passion in anybody's eyes. Do not be just another fish in the pond. Make sure that you *live* it."

"Yeah man, you got to dig your own way out. Just make sure you use the right shovel." Brian said and winked at him, "Meet you at the top, then."

"Have a blast, goodbye!" Matilda said, as they walked out into the crowd.

"You too!" He shouted, smiling. He had never met such an enlightening couple. *The night wasn't a waste, at all, just the foundation.*

- x -

XIV

It was her last working day. The past two days had passed, as she would recall, in a rather low-key manner, much to her disappointment; helping out and attending to the very few customers, three to be accurate, and answering phone-calls and e-mails and some paper-work. But, nonetheless, she was happy at her one accomplishment whence she had managed to sell a set of very luxurious and rather expensive (which she had found out only later, much to her surprise) drawing room chairs; not a whole set of furniture but two rather exotic chairs. The gentleman who bought them didn't at all resemble a collector, not that collectors had a certain stereotype, but this man had the air of a bored office executive who appeared least interested in buying such expensive antiques after a long office day. Maybe, she conjectured he was from some museum; now that was something!

She had duly booked it under the customer's name, a Mr. Bakshi. The actual proceedings would be handled later by the owner, who had been kept updated over the phone and who was pretty impressed, after she returned. The lady was supposed to return that very night. She was suddenly reminded that it was a matter of just a few more hours till her work would be done; and to add to it, she would receive her pay too! It was the only spark of excitement in an otherwise dull morning which she had mostly passed in meditation as there was not much work to be done and zero customers.

Soon it was afternoon and by then she was almost sitting and twiddling her thumbs, waiting for the day to end. She had finished exploring the store in the past two days as she had ample time but had found nothing *extraordinaire*. This dampened all her imaginative thoughts which soon lost their appeal. The few unusual items that had intrigued her in the beginning turned out to hold no special charm, only plain difference in appearance, just that.

Six fifteen. She was aware of the sun setting outside, a magnificent sunset no doubt, and it was almost time to close down. These last few days they had closed down at 6 pm sharp, but today they would remain open till the return of the owner, perhaps by 6:30, as she had informed them.

Lyla suddenly heard the tinkling sound of the door bell and for a second thought that the owner had arrived early, but then was somewhat surprised to see a young man entering, *not a regular feature in an Antique shop, that too all by himself.*

The young man, upon entering, first looked around, trying to absorb the surroundings much like she herself had done when she had come in for the very first time. Probably a newcomer, she guessed, observing his actions. Then he turned towards the counter where she was sitting and said something which suddenly caught her off-guard,

"Strange interest! Antiques. Really, how long have you been indulging in it? Though looking at you, it seems otherwise."

All this while he pretended to keep a straight face, as though he meant business but she was aware inwardly that he was definitely mocking her.

"Excuse me? I...um...am the manager here," she said, but seeing him intently looking at her, with tilted head, she added, "I mean temporarily because the owner's out of town. And then again what did you mean by "looking at me it seems otherwise?" she looked straight at him.

He seemed not much older than she was, probably in his early twenties and something about him seemed, *mysteriously cute.*

It seems he found something funny because he let out a small laugh and said smiling, "I figured."

"What? What are you saying...wait, why are you even here? Definitely not to just talk?" she faked anger but she was intrigued.

Then she closed her eyes and opening them again went into the businesslike mode that she had learnt these past couple of days and said, "So, are you interested in any specific piece? You can look around but please be quick because we are closing shortly."

All this while he had been looking at her as if she was something interesting. When he had walked into the store he had never expected something like this, really what can you expect in a dull Antiques store?

But he was really surprised to see *her*, sitting there all by herself, trying to appear professional, despite her air of inexperience that was so evident in that pretty face. *Probably a student, still in college, temporary job, Whoa..those big eyes are appealing, especially when she changes her composure, nice try!*

Again he made that straight face and said, "No, I'm just looking around though nothing has caught my attention yet," then a sudden smile, a curving of the mouth, "but I have a feeling it has begun to", and winked.

His gesture startled her, making her blush but she still maintained her composure and said in a professional voice, "But I am afraid you've got to hurry as we are about to close shop." Staring at her watch she saw that it was 6.35, the owner would be there any minute.

"In a hurry yourself, are you?" he said, noticing her anxious glances at the watch.

But before she could reply, the front door opened and the owner entered, looking tired from a long journey, carrying a bag. Then looking at the two of them standing there she said, "Hello, I'm back, and so glad!" and addressing the boy said, "Eeshaan, good to see you here finally!"

"Aunt Tara, you are back. How are things there?" he said.

"Yeah, yeah, things are pretty much okay. Resolved now." She replied, "Oh for a glass of water!" which the shop assistant diligently presented her with.

The sudden exchanges and the familiarity

astonished Lyla. What was going on, were the boy and the lady acquaintances, relatives even?

Then the lady turned to her and said, "Well, thank you Lyla, I mean, really, for helping me out here," and shaking her hand said smiling, "Pretty impressive job skills."

It was nice to watch her shed that serious tone for once. Then looking at the boy the woman said, "I had told, Eeshaan here, to check in at least once while I was out and he comes in now when I'm back already."

"I'm sorry", he said shrugging his shoulders, "I was really busy."

"Yes, yes, always busy with your music. When will you do something constructive?"

Music? Was he some kind of Musician?

"Aunty, I've got to go now. I'm in a hurry." he said, about to leave.

"Wait. Hey, see-off this young lady to her place. It's getting dark and not so safe out there. The least I can do."

"No, no need. I can go on my own." Lyla tried to say.

"But..." they both spoke at the same time, but the lady shushed them off. "It's an order."

....

They walked side by side down the sidewalk, silently. None of the easy conversations, the flirting banter and the laughter of the past was there. They were both almost introspective, lost in their thoughts.

After a few paces, she spoke up, "Hey, thanks, really..I can go on my own."

"You see the way everything looks now. Slowly daylight is giving in to darkness, the dark being more dominant. There is this alluring mixture of light and shadows; something mysterious, something unexplainable, the best of twilight. The perfect medley." he said instead.

As he spoke, she looked at him hard, a strange look of interest in her face; while he seemed lost, in his own world.

After a while, she spoke up, "City streets, life in concrete; where dreams galore in materialistic needs. Past the glitter, past all the rushing cars therein lingers a rhythm, maybe tonight I can write a song for you."

He was totally caught off-guard by her response and looked at her, amusement etched on his face. He shook his head before he spoke up, as if to find words to say, "That was amazing! You are a Songwriter? I mean, it's rough but it sure is something!"

She was smiling too; amused herself but she shook her head and said shyly, "No."

"No? But I think if you try, you sure can, you know, become one." He said.

She was still smiling, "Are you a..uh, a musician?"

"I don't know, I love music and I'm just trying my hand at different genres." He said.

"That's pretty cool, I guess."

"Maybe, but at the end of the day, it's like, I haven't found my own place, you know, the place where we all belong."

She nodded, "I know the feeling."

****

That night, as she went to bed, she couldn't help thinking about the walk back home with *him*; a total stranger that he was, but she felt in that brief time she could almost understand him. *Maybe she was thinking too much, this was not a movie!*

She had not wanted the evening to end, wanted that walk to be never-ending, but reality stared right in her face. As they reached her place and they stood at the gate, he bade goodbye, "We both have a long way to go then."

"Yes, find our true calling. Bye, see you, maybe."

"Maybe" and waved, "Bye." That slow smile. Oh!

-   x   -

XV

Months passed, seasons changed and lives progressed. He embarked on his journey looking for music, while she was busy with college. But she never forgot him. He too remembered her but what kept coming back was her lyrical prowess. And she too gave vent to it, indulging in it whenever she really could. Soon it was the last year of her college life. As for him, his year and a half after college which he had asked for, to prove his mettle in music to his parents or otherwise pack-up and go for higher studies, was coming to an end as it was nearly December! But he had not yet been able to find his foothold and was losing all hope, and on the verge of giving up and going for studies abroad.

****

It was a quiet December morning. The sun shone bright but there was an inherent chill in the air, not too much nor too less, yet something that didn't keep the woolens at bay. He was still in bed when his phone rang. It was his playwright friend, Abhimanyu, who wanted him to come over to Mandi House, a place in New Delhi. There was this certain Sri Ram Centre for Performing Arts where one of his plays would be staged that afternoon. He had taken to direction after a hiatus and this play was special because he had written as well as directed it. Thus he didn't want his best friends to miss it; but since Arden was out of town as usual and Jeff had an important day at the restaurant, he wanted at least Eeshaan to be there.

Now theatre was not his thing, though he had enjoyed watching plays back in college and had even tried his hand at the background score once in Abhimanyu's own play, but nevertheless, he agreed to go so as to be there for his friend on his important day.

....

He drove to the location and on arriving, went

directly backstage. Abhimanyu was somewhat nervous. Seeing his best friend all jittery before his big event brought a smile to Eeshaan's face and he went and hugged him hard, wishing him luck. Then he entered the auditorium and found his seat at the back.

The play was about to start, the props were all arranged, the curtains were up and the character on stage although static now would start as soon as the music was played. Just as the earlier dim lights were brightened and the first notes of the piano filled the auditorium, someone came rushing in through the door all of a sudden. Eeshaan was startled as he was sitting right next to the door. He saw a young woman, muttering something to herself before saying out loud, "Shit, I'm late!" She then settled down in the empty seat just next to him.

"How much have I missed?" she addressed him suddenly.

"It has just began, you haven't missed much", he replied.

"Good. Thought I would never make it, oh these Delhi jams!" she said, not looking at him, her eyes stuck on the stage; as if speaking to herself.

He looked at her. She was pretty in an unconventional sort of way but she looked nothing like a theatre enthusiast, not that theatre and art lovers had a stereotype, but she seemed better suited to corporate business meetings or black tie dinners perhaps, with very short straight hair and oxblood red lipstick, no earrings he noticed. She had this air or so he observed, and before he could stop himself he asked out loud, "Do you know Abhimanyu or are you really a theatre enthusiast?"

She didn't reply immediately, being engrossed in the play, and only managed a "What?" and giving him a totally blank look said, "I'm sorry, did you say something?"

"Nothing" he shook his head, deciding to mind his own business.

....

After the play was over, as he stood and chatted with his playwright friend and a few actors and some other people, someone, perhaps from the audience, interrupted them, apologizing in a way that seemed sort of businesslike. It was the same young lady he had encountered earlier. She addressed Abhimanyu and congratulated him, praising him to an extent that made Eeshaan raise an eyebrow and give her a speculative look, but Abhimanyu seemed pleased and was openly blushing.

"I have also seen your previous play in Connaught Place, which was in March, I guess, and that's when I became such a fan and when I got to know that another one of your plays was being staged here, I knew I had to see it" she said.

"Oh really, you saw "The unfinished verse", that's really nice...thanks!" Abhimanyu smiled. Then, not knowing what to say, he turned to his friend and said, "Why, here, he too was a part of it, he took care of the music."

Eeshaan looked at his friend with narrowed eyes, but was forced to smile when she said to him, "Oh

71

did you; why yes, we've met already earlier today, right?" only then did she seem to notice him.

"Yeah right", he replied.

Just then as if remembering something she added, "And yeah, my cousin strangely seemed to like your music then, I mean, the background score", he was all ears but she gave a small laugh and said, "Actually that's all that she liked about the play, not a theatre person."

"Hey wait, I remember, I remember we did have a small chat then didn't we? In CP[2]?" Abhimanyu seemed to recall their previous meeting.

"Yes we did, I'm glad that you remember!" she said beaming.

"Actually, I'm so sorry that I forgot." he said blushing.

"Tell your cousin, I appreciate that" Eeshaan said cutting in.

"Okay" but all her interest was in the playwright, who seemed just as interested too.

"Hey, are you up for a cup of coffee?" she offered.

"Yes, I would love to!" he said.

Something was definitely brewing between them. "I should get going now", Eeshaan said, "Later, man!" The two friends shook hands and he turned to leave.

Turning, Eeshaan almost bumped into someone, some girl, and they both muttered apologies at the same time and looked at each other.

"Hi", she said, recognition dawning in her look.

---

[2] Connaught Place, New Delhi

"Hey!" he definitely knew her, of course, it was *her*, "Songwriter, What are you doing here?"

But before she could reply, "You have met my cousin then?" the other woman said.

"What..?" he looked from her to the other woman.

"I'm here to pick up my cousin, after which we are both headed home", she said, and then addressing her cousin, "Maya, I was waiting for you outside but since you took so long..."

"Lyla, I'm sorry.." her cousin replied, and giving her an apologetic look said, "I shall not be going home right now, you see..." and looked at the playwright as if to explain.

Things seemed to make sense, after all Maya was intrigued by the same guy they had met in CP, "Okay, I got it...so, have fun then."

"Hey songwriter!" *he* said to *her*, "If you are not in a hurry to leave, how about both of us hanging out for a while?"

"Oh, that would be nice, but I have to leave." She said somewhat reluctantly.

"Okay. Curfew?" he asked.

"No, no...actually I've got to pack", and seeing his questioning look, "We're going away for the weekend."

"Oh really, Cool! Okay then" he said almost biding adieu.

"Yeah, just the two of us," she said pointing to her cousin, who in turn said, "Hey, why don't you guys join us too, it will be fun, I mean if you are free."

"What?" she threw a startled look at her cousin, who seemed serious and said, "what?" as if it was nothing unusual.

"Why not? We would love to, right dude?" Eeshaan said, all excited.

"Yeah, I guess so", Abhimanyu was somewhat unsure but eager, "Yes."

"But we hardly know one another!" She said, "I'm sorry, but I don't know if it's a good idea."

"Then it's the best way to get to know one another", he replied.

"I agree", Maya concluded leaving no room for further argument.

Lyla didn't seem to mind, for a change, it felt curiously good. Eeshaan was himself surprised at his audacity yet he needed a break and meeting her all over again, it seemed to hit a familiar essence.

-   x   -

XVI

That trip, as she remembered later, was one of those few moments in life whence one loses oneself to bring out the best within. She would definitely brand it as one of the best experiences of her life, given she had a journal. It started off as a little insecure in the beginning, as they drove away from the metropolitan fast lanes marred by traffic onto the outskirts complemented by nature, quiet and keeping to itself. As civilization was replaced by the canopy of trees on the roadside and shades of green became dominant while the mountain caricatures could be traced on the borderline, the atmosphere was transformed. None but *he* was the first one to break the ice when he started humming along with the music playing in the car and it turned out that he was a huge Nirvana fan which she had already figured out when they had talked about their favorite Artistes. The Playwright it seemed had a penchant for filmmaking and he discussed ideas for a road movie to which her cousin listened intently, and being an avid reader, put in her opinions by touching upon her favorite road novels. By the time they reached the narrow winding roads that led to the picturesque hill station, they were laughing loudly like old friends, mocking at their own selves for taking a trip to a hill-station in winter and squirming in the cold!

The cold breeze and the chill in the air;
Wrapped up in sweaters and heavy denims to beat the cold;
Seeking a peaceful moment amid the hustle-bustle;
Though the spirit of poetry lingers in the air, trying hard to rhyme![3]

"Snowfall is Nature's own decoration of Mother Earth", Eeshaan observed.

They journeyed amongst the hills blanketed by moving clouds, along the winding roads, peeked at the occasional waterfalls. With the daunting mountainous topography and the specks of

---

[3] Poetry from my blog: The Rearview.

civilization amidst it, nature was at her best.

"It's like a dream, such poetic bliss in the air!" Lyla said, awed by what she saw.

Later on, their long walks, taking in the little market, checking out souvenirs, tasting the local cuisine, a real delicacy; the endless talk, the laughter and the local-sightseeing; it was just the two of them hanging out. There were jokes, there were insights, there were interests; she had never had a conversation of that sort with anyone before. With the other two blooming love-birds away for the most part, they both hung out a lot together. He seemed to have so much passion, she harbored an unknowing admiration that reflected in the way she looked at him but he was too busy to notice, too caught up in his own convictions, and it was then that she realized her own inherent hidden love for music.

....

That Sunday, the last night of their stay, they both sat on the grass outside, he straddled with his guitar, strumming a few incoherent notes once in a while, and she typically engrossed in her task of writing a few lines of a song. It was a starry night, quiet, unlike the city, so quiet that it seemed unusual. They used flashlights as she read out her lines and he tried to set them to music. They were giggling like carefree teenagers. At that very moment she was so happy, and for once in her life she really felt free and alive.

She wanted to shout out loud! Well, for a change somebody understood her and shared the same insatiable craziness! That night as they would recall later, was *legendary* in the sense that unknowingly they both discovered themselves.

"It's always been music for me, those gruesome teenage years when I realized my calling" he was meditative all of a sudden, "Though it started off as a coping mechanism initially, it became a passion with time."

"Is it going to be the same in the future too?" she asked.

"Music will always be there in my life, regardless of what I end up doing", he said and added with a grin, "Though I'm not sure where I'll really end up!"

"Why? Won't you be pursuing music? I mean isn't it your career already?" she was surprised by his response.

"Well, when it comes to reality, you cannot make a career out of your passion, which I got to learn the hard way, only in books do they manage to fool you!" he said laughing, more at himself.

Then noticing that thoughtful searching look on her face as she didn't join in that self-mocking laughter, he explained, "Just after I finished my graduation, I decided to take a year off to harness my passion into something constructive at which I failed immensely, and so as the new year sets in, I'll have to pack my bags and head abroad for further studies as part of this deal with my parents."

"Oh..." that's all she could manage.

"Yeah, that's me in the future; probably I'll end up

stuffed up in some office room, stuck in a daily 9 to 5 job and overwork on Sundays, no life, much like a robot!" He strummed his guitar hard, playing some really high notes.

"What is the other option?" she said.

"What other option?" He looked at her questioningly.

"If you did succeed in your endeavor, you know, if you did manage to establish a career out of your passion" she said.

"I don't know...looking at it seems so useless now..." he said brooding and added, "And I'm the least interested in studying some goddamn technical course!"

After a pause she said, "I'm graduating too next year, you know, and I'm pretty clueless about what to pursue...but then I have this crazy idea in my head right now."

"Really, how crazy?" he smiled.

"Hear me out. What if, what if we both collaborated, you know, I write songs and you sing them and we make music, totally completely different, like we have our own label!" she sounded so excited.

"Don't be silly. That's really crazy. Not possible." He ignored the idea forthright.

"No! Why not? Think about it!" She was almost persistent.

"No, it ain't that easy" he said.

"How can you be so rational being a musician?" she said, her eyes wide.

Eeshaan chuckled, "That's funny. Now let's get all

those ideas out of your head okay. Let's call it a night."

"What? No! Listen you can't go for something you don't want to, you'll lose everything! What about following your heart?" She could almost stamp her foot.

"Those are big ideas and like I said only in books, doesn't happen in reality." He said.

"Hey, what are you two arguing about?" it was Maya back from a stroll with Abhimanyu.

They both shook their heads, "Nothing"

"Wasn't it such an amazing weekend?" Maya exclaimed.

"Yeah and I think we should do this more often, right guys?" Abhimanyu said.

"Yes."

"Lyla, you had fun with him, no?" Maya addressed her cousin.

"I had a really great time, best" She smiled at Eeshaan, "Made me re-think things, about life" and winked at him.

At which he shrugged and looked away, a smile switched on his face.

Early next morning they drove back to the city, away from nature's abode tucked away in tradition and returned to commitments, to reality. It was like they had moved away from the light and taken shelter in the shadows again.

****

Soon the old year ended and a brand new one kicked

in. The whole world partied till they were wasted and as January walked in with much pomp and celebration, Lyla couldn't help thinking about Eeshaan, *what did he do of himself? Did he really set off abroad abandoning his passion? If so, how could he?* After that day, parting ways at the doorstep, they made a strange pact of not exchanging any form of contact details, *"Let's rely on fate and see if it makes us meet again"*. She had thought about it first and he had agreed. She had wanted to keep it as surreal as possible. *What if serendipity did sprinkle some magic into their lives?* She wondered. But the thought of him going away, indulging in something which he hated, made her feel bad for him and she made a resolution that no matter what, she'd start writing songs and try and pursue her lyrical skills. *Maybe we should have exchanged numbers. If only he would call.* Now that her cousin and his friend were officially dating they knew that they could reach each other easily, but they chose not to.

-   x   -

XVII

The London air didn't seem to suit him. He hated the cold, hated the constant rain and didn't enjoy the campus life at his University. Classes didn't interest him and he found the lectures boring. Despite the varied activities on campus, life seemed dull and somber and he couldn't help reminiscing about his graduation days where he had the time and the heart to indulge in creativity and fun. He rarely played his guitar, only once in a while to cut out stress; and the days felt as gloomy as the weather.

All this while, *her* words of that night at the hill station kept lingering in the back of his mind. Most nights when he was frustrated with the current state of his life, those lines kept nagging him, *What if he was brave enough to take one chance.* But he shoved them off, calling it rubbish.

....

It was a fine February Sunday despite the cold and for once he had the pleasure of curling up in bed and reading. Just two pages of a gritty detective novel and his eyelids kept drooping and soon enough he was nodding off. But he was awoken at once by somebody banging hard on his door.

Against his better judgment he wanted to shout out loud, "Go away!" But he decided against it and instead got out of bed to open the door to his classmate and new-found friend Tim who was beaming from ear to ear and said in his Australian accent, "Rise and shine, mate! It's time to party!"

"I don't have time to party." He said in a rather bored voice.

"No, no, I'm not talking about the usual night club bonhomie. This is different and I have an inkling that you'll like it." Tim said, holding out what seemed like two passes.

"What are these?" he said taking them.

The Universal Incognito Creative Society welcomes you to a MUSICAL NIGHT like no other. Entry only by passes. Tonight @10.00. Venue: You know where, so see you there!

"What is *this*!?" he exclaimed, looking questioningly at his friend but his eyes gleaming with a tinge of curiosity.

"This is *the* thing. We can't afford to miss it, man!" Tim said faking a serious look.

Eeshaan looked at the passes again and stood there staring at them for a while.

And then with a grin on his face said, "Let's not miss it then!"

....

The night was magical and it felt as if the stars had come down to earth, aligning themselves over the water, balancing against the dark reins of boredom and for once illuminating life!

There were so many lights everywhere! Hanging onto the dark, laying into the nowhere! From tree branches and boat houses to rooftops and masts of old broken ferries. Walking down the old unused dock, it was a sight to behold. There on the sole ship, abandoned and retired from its glory days of cruising on the high seas, was a party like no other! There were all sorts of people, in all sorts of dresses, appearances and the like! There was food and there were drinks and there was music, all of the *right* kind.

Oh the music was out of the world! He had never experienced so many different types and genres of music ever, or seen so much passion and dedication to an Art! It was like he had walked through the old wardrobe into Narnia! Or flown in with the storm and landed into the Land of Oz! It seemed other-worldly, the whole ambience. There were psychedelics, the goods that destroyed karma, smokers and drinkers, creative slaves and prisoners and all rode the bandwagon to freedom, the call for life. Some others seemed to have lost it, giving in completely to their Art! It was creepily crazy yet mesmerizing to the core!

He felt too damn plain in his jeans and jacket while vibrant dressers with the weirdest of hairstyles and the most unique outfits thronged the party. It seemed there were people from all over the world, speaking in different languages with varied accents.

There was even a hall of fame of sorts in one of the cabins! Portraits were hung under the title 'Gods of Music' and there were the Beatles, David Bowie, Bob Dylan, Elton John among others, and beyond that a wall where there were signatures of all the legends themselves, everyone from Black Sabbath, The Who, to The Doors and The Eagles! It seemed they had visited this mad fairyland themselves at some time or the other. There were also messages from contemporary musicians Coldplay, One Republic and the Mumford and Sons! On another wall, Ed Sheraan had penned down some lyrics on a piece of paper and there were self notes from Joan Jett, Elli

Goulding, and Pink among others! It seemed everyone from Massive Attack, Maroon 5 to the Zac Brown Band, Paramore, Shania Twain to The Lumineers, and Green Day had been there! The place was plain crazy!

But the venue had no airs, everyone was equal there. Anyone, everyone with a passion for creativity was welcome there. But it was a very secret private event, invitation only by passes. He couldn't help thinking how Tim could have access to a place like this!

There was one rule to the club, as Tim explained later, established musicians never performed, it gave the opportunity to the new, struggling talents. It was rumored that some contemporary musicians who had made it big were first discovered here. But the place strictly prohibited commercialism and hence the media had never discovered it. Only trusted music producers were allowed there who promised to preserve the anonymity of the place and only visited it just as individuals with a love for music. It was even believed that celebrities were made to sign some Non Disclosure Agreement (NDA) before visiting the place.

This Musical event was held only once a year in different locations all over the world, in different countries, across continents. As for the rest, there was also a Writers Club, an arts exhibition and all sorts of creativity related events held at some point of time or the other. The coming together of people with the same eccentric urges for creativity under one roof, or in this case on board an old ship! It all seemed ethereal and made Eeshaan think and question. As realization came in with the dawn he felt metaphorically awoken.

After days of slumber, so long have you been sleeping?

- x -

XVIII

The next morning his head was fuzzy from the lack of sleep and the drinking. Though he was not completely hung-over, he had a slight nagging headache. As he sat there, he popped an Advil and gulped some water and looked into the distance. He could see the countless automobiles plying on the London Bridge from where he sat on the park bench. It was the 'rush hour' and life seemed to be in motion, leaving him alone. He felt as if he had been sitting there since eternity, breathing in life, living; the freshness of the morning on his face, the sun shining brightly and he was least worried about missing classes, completing assignments, or finding jobs. He was just happy, in the moment, because he knew and he was not afraid, not anymore.

Coming back from the party at 6 in the morning, they were all groggy but he was thoughtful. He did not accompany Tim back to the hostel, but instead had decided to walk, just walk, at least *walk away* from it all.

Strolling along thinking, he had made a decision that very morning. It was not easy, but he knew he had to do it. Just as it is said, *'it is now or never.'*

Now sitting there overlooking the London Bridge, indulging in the freshness of the morning, he was happy and for once in days he felt alive.

....

Exactly a week later, he flew back to India, leaving behind London and his Masters degree in Development Studies. His parents were naturally disappointed but eventually gave in. His explanation more or less convinced them and they decided to support his decision and back him up, after all he was their only son and more importantly, they sensed a change in him. It seemed Eeshaan was no longer the lost, carefree youngster but a determined person. *He had so needed that London chapter!*

....

March was spent in preparations. It was her end term final exams. Yet she was so unsure about what lay ahead of her post examinations. She would be graduating that summer and unlike the past years when she was so sure of what she wanted to do, this time she was clueless. It was as if she had shed her practical, mechanical self and was looking out onto the horizon armed with curiosity and passion. *She needed to find her true calling.*

As for him, he was gearing up for something big.

....

Strangely enough, one fine spring day, he found himself visiting the same small hill station which they had traversed last winter. Roaming along the streets alone, he recalled the events of December and smiled at the memories. Strolling absent mindedly, he reached the other end of the town, which was unfamiliar to him, but seemed somewhat deserted except for a few postcard-pretty houses. However, what caught his eye was that amidst all the dolled-up prettiness stood a rather unusual looking structure. At first sight it resembled an old office-building but the top floor seemed a little out of place.

As he stood there observing it, somebody spoke from behind all of a sudden, startling him.

"This old place, it does seem to stand out even after all these years."

It was an elderly man. But he seemed like a *foreigner*, he had the Caucasian features of a European.

The man smiled and continued, "Back in the day, it was the place we called home, the place which was freedom, the place where we made our music."

The dramatic manner of the man interested him and he curiously asked, "Made music?"

"Yes, those days, the 70s, it was the only place we let it loose, cut-off from the world, no worries, just peace and music, ah!" The man said.

By then he was staring at the older person who sounded more like an American.

"It was our studio back in our glory days" said the man smiling nostalgically.

"Anyway, I'm Sam," the man said holding out his hand to Eeshaan, "I bet you're wondering who I am. I'm a globetrotter who keeps coming back to this wonderful little place" he said and added winking, "The world is my home, and I'm a hopeless wanderer, you can call me a global citizen but what I really am is a king of the road!"

He stared at the man in awe and admiration, *so much passion for life!* and said, "Whoa, I'm really intrigued!"

"I know. You young people need to live a little" and giving him a pat on the shoulder said, "Okay, later young man" and left.

"Sure Sir." He couldn't help wondering at the audacity of the man.

All this while, a new, rather interesting, idea crept into his mind and the thought of it made him smile. He had discovered the best possible thing and he thought, *this was it.*

Standing there he wanted to shout out loud. God, Life can be really surprising!

-   x -

XIX

March was in its last week, almost over, and the

smell of warm summer with reminders of the threatening scorching Delhi heat wafted up in the air! She thought, *Oh spring, it will be gone so fast!* She sat, musing over the book of Shakespeare's Plays, on the balcony overlooking the green lawn below and the high trees on the periphery of their compound walls. She was still deep in thought when her phone buzzed. An unknown number flashed on the screen. Though a little reluctant, she received the call anyway, only to hear a shrill female voice on the other end who addressed her by her first name. She was a little surprised at this sudden display of familiarity and assumed it was some old friend, till the person at the other end said, "You probably don't know me but I'm Saudamini and I'm calling from the Lost Harmonica records label, you know, the one newly launched by the Blue Ivy Group?"

"Wait. Records label?" She was totally confused.

"Yes." The other person replied.

"Why are you calling me?" she asked.

"You see, this is a special request from our new Recording Artist whom we'll be launching soon and who also happens to be our first," she sounded rather excited, "and he wants you in his team."

She was too surprised to speak till realization slowly seemed to dawn on her, a sense of familiar excitement at some memory, but then it was not possible, *and how could it be?* No. No. Maybe it was a prank call.

As if sensing her thoughts, the girl on the other end said, "This is no practical joke. We are calling you from the Lost Harmonica Records for real. You can cross-check the number, it's in our website."

But she interrupted the speaker midway and said, "This Artist in question, can I have a word with him please, provided it is okay."

"It sure is okay, but I'm afraid you won't be able to reach him right now. But you can take his personal number or we'll let him know so that he can call you." The girl said.

"Okay thanks, but I need to go now. Later then."

"Okay, sure," said the cheerful voice, "Have a good day ahead."

Ending the call, a string of thoughts ran through her mind and she said out loud, "What the hell? What the hell, really!"

First, she hadn't heard from him in days, he had left so damn fast, not even a goodbye message (yes they had agreed on a no communications pact but..), no clue of his current status, nothing. Last December when she had tried to talk him into following his passion, he had rubbished her and now out of the blue she gets some unknown call from some big shot Records Label that they want to hire her because some 'Recording Artist', yeah that's definitely *him*, wants her on his team! Doesn't he have the nerve to call her up himself cutting out all the professional shit! This was all so crazy!

Her spirits were in a flutter, a mixture of emotions engulfed her all at once and she was so overwhelmed that she slammed her book shut and stormed into her bedroom.

Her last exam was on the 30th of that month and then entrances in April. She was in the middle of her final year exams! Soon she would have to apply for Masters in a couple of Universities in the country itself. It was the busiest week of the year for her and this was hardly the time to be bestowed with 'surprises', adding further fuel to the fire of complexities in life!

As these thoughts lingered in her mind during the course of the day, she was left to battle with mixed feelings. There were no further calls. So by the end of the day she tried to forget about it all, but in vain. It was no joke; she had checked the website and rechecked it too in the commercial phonebook. Was it not something that which she really wanted? Did she really want to attend some University, get involved in some Masters program majoring in English? Yes she liked the subject and had always had a flair for literature, but it was not what she wanted. In the last two months, since that December trip, she had discovered a real passion for writing songs, she felt like she had dug up a rare treasure that had been hidden for centuries in her backyard, had experienced that feeling of pure joy and great excitement. It was as if she had found the missing link that made her life more than just ordinary, adding a real spark to it, lighting it up like a firework and in the process she had found her real self; probably stumbled upon her fate, *her destiny?*

Thinking about it, it all made so much sense, like it was all she had ever wanted. She wanted to become a songwriter.

Engrossed in such deep meditation, contemplating, reflecting upon things, indulging in an inner debate, she realized secretly that this was what she really wanted and waited for was a call from *him,* though outwardly she behaved as if she had given up on the matter at hand, on him.

What if it was not him? A sudden thought struck her; maybe some other person. 'Would she find the same bone-chilling excitement in collaborating with, writing songs for someone else, anyone else other than him?'

And she realized, it was more than just songwriting, the person in question also played a major role in her dream. Was it because he was the first person to acknowledge her talent and encourage her? Absolutely, *what else could be the reason?*

And she beamed at the memory of the times, though so fleeting, that they had spent together, especially in that hill station, for she now realized that she really liked him.

It was almost midnight but there were no calls. Lyla waited and waited, sleepless, triggered by a heightened sense of anticipation; excitement that turned to anxiety and finally she was almost disheartened. The next morning she woke to the notion that it was just two days to her last exam. *Enough of mere fantasy, she had her life and career to consider!*

- x -

XX

By the end of March, he had most of the arrangements completed. The renowned Blue Ivy Group agreed to launch him under their new Records Label, Lost Harmonica; it was only by sheer coincidence that they had decided to invest in the music industry. How he had grabbed the deal was another story.

On the last Sunday of February after his return, he had received a call from his friend Jeff asking him to come over to his restaurant immediately. Eeshaan was confused but he had gone anyway.

"Hey, over here!" Jeff called out as Eeshaan walked into the artistically crafted restaurant where the former worked as the head chef. He walked over to where his friend was sitting with a lady who seemed British.

"Hi. What's the matter?" he asked.

"Hey, meet Sarah Anderson from London." Jeff said instead.

"Hello, you must be the musician?" the lady said, "Please take a seat."

"Maybe..." He was so surprised that he looked at his friend questioningly and caught his smile. Then he held out his hand to her and shook it saying simply, "Hello, I'm Eeshaan."

"Sarah works in the music scene back in London and she's here in India for some research." Jeff said.

"It's more of hunting for some investment in this country." She winked and gave a small laugh.

She looked old enough to be in her 50's and she had the air of a professional. Still he was confused.

"And yes, she and her team are hosting a party

93

here tomorrow for the Blue Ivy group, more of a business thing." Jeff said.

"You must be wondering how your friend here has so much information. Well, my husband is also in India, and he happens to really like the food here and so we have hired Mr. Ellis as a chef for the 'South Asian Entrée' which is based in Amsterdam and headed by my husband."

"Oh really, that is great news, Jeff!" He congratulated his friend.

"Well, Mr. Ellis informed me about you when I told him that I work in the music scene but since you have left London already I won't be of much help." Then she smiled and continued, "But I happen to know that the Blue Ivy Group has some plans for this genre and just like you I'm interested too, though for different reasons." She said.

"Pardon me, I couldn't quite get you." He said.

"We want to extend our records label, 'Lost Harmonica' to India and we want an Indian company to head and invest in it and the Blue Ivy Group is just perfect for the same, hence the party tomorrow." She said.

"This is interesting." He said.

....

On Tuesday morning he got a call from Sarah herself.

"Yes Lost Harmonica is in India, and for goodness's sake, they already are launching a new Artist. Congratulations!"

He was overjoyed and thanked her profusely.

Things seemed to be falling into place now. For

once he felt lucky. But luck was not the real factor behind the lady's decision to just launch him on Jeff's word alone, without even listening to his work.

Only later did he find out that it was actually three of his best friends who were responsible for it. It was Arden who had met the lady's husband on several of his trips, and recommended Jeff to him. The man who had Indian roots had agreed to look into Jeff's work while on his tour to India with his wife, who was going there on business to seal a music deal. Arden had then consulted Abhimanyu who happened to have had a few of Eeshaan's music at hand, and they had sent it to Sarah. Jeff, while hosting the couple had spoken to them about Eeshaan, and as they were relishing his food had arranged the meeting. He was immensely grateful to his friends and this time he really thanked his luck for their friendship.

Now that he had a secure deal, Eeshaan was able to set foot on the more difficult part of the work. The process was not easy and took him almost a month to start on his musical journey. But he had his heart set on it and it felt completely worth it.

....

All this while, he had not forgotten about *her*, and if there was one thing he was sure of, it was of her being on his team as a songwriter. He was quite excited about the way things were turning out and had wanted to contact her right away, but then remembering the way he had forthright rejected her idea last December, he needed to make sure that he was on a firm footing before he could call her on board. Through Maya, who was now in a relationship with Abhimanyu, he had come to know about Lyla's on-going examinations and had decided to wait until she was done with them before calling her up and letting her know. In the meantime he'd be done with the arrangements.

He was really upset with the record company's sudden call to her the previous day as he had wanted to be the first one to break the news to her, but then again such matters were not on his hands. However, when they informed him that Lyla had agreed to comply but only after a word with him, he was both relieved and excited all at once, because he was aware that she had figured that it was him after all. So in her best interests, he had decided to wait until she was free before contacting her.

. . . .

April came both fast and slow. Though Lyla's examinations were over, she was burdened by a sense of melancholy. It was the 2nd of April and nobody had contacted her yet. Her entrances were next week and she had half a mind to skip them due to the uncertainty.

-   x   -

XXI

Bombay was beautiful. There was the sea, the glistening beach in its peculiar patterns, and then there was the city. A touch of historical colonial legacy in its architecture amalgamated with the essence of present day modernity, cosmopolitanism being the defining element. Though it was now called Mumbai, the old sense of the term still prevailed among its inhabitants. As is depicted in our own Bollywood films, the historic railway station, Chatrapati Shivaji Terminus, is focused as the gateway to the city of dreams, *India's own L.A.*; and then the glimpses of the city's iconic landmarks and the busy streets along the un-ending skyscrapers, a spot on Marine Drive, all welcoming the starry-eyed nobody to the big life.

Cities did not appeal to him, having grown up in New Delhi. He longed for the quiet life of small towns and he was well aware that a certain pretty little hill station was the place for him, like Sam had so perfectly put it, "just music and peace".

He was on a hasty visit to Mumbai, where the Records Label was actually based, to convince the 'bosses', the executive producers, to let him set up his own working base at the studio in the hill-station. Through local sources he had found out that the studio was up for sale and they needed to act fast before somebody else got their hands on it and demolished it.

It had been a tiring day, spent in closed door meetings and boring conversations and it made him realize that he was not cut out for the corporate stuff!

Later that night, the city glittered, a plethora of lights with a scenic skyline. As he lay down on his comfortable bed in his hotel room, he heaved a sigh of relief that the long day was over. He was a little optimistic about the verdict the next day and crossed his fingers at the thought. He opened his calendar app to look up some dates and suddenly realized it was the 6th of April already, almost a week had passed and he was yet to call *her*. He immediately dialed the number, so eagerly saved from earlier, despite the time which read 23:55. The call went to voicemail instead as it was indicated that the phone was switched-off. *Shit*, he was suddenly apprehensive but decided to skip it and give it another try in the morning. He didn't leave any messages.

****

As her friend drove her to the University Building, she was a little nervous about the interview; but more than that she was confused. Her mind was embroiled in an inner conflict, a part of her wanted to run away and not apply to the Master's degree in the University. Outside, looking through the car window, the city was beautiful. The neo-gothic British era architecture of the old buildings amalgamating with the modern day structures, stood out, adding a unique touch and feel to the city. She had chosen Mumbai, a change of place, perhaps a change in life situations too, but was she really looking forward to it?

Her friend dropped her off at the main gate and wishing her luck, drove away.

After that she just stood there in front of the gate, looking through the bars at the rush of people inside, students and other individuals coming in and going out; with bags and books in hand, everyone busy shaping their lives, following their dreams and she thought, *Dreams, what about them?* Shouldn't she follow hers too?

'I'm in Mumbai, look around me, it's the place to which people come from all aspects of life to find their destiny and strangely enough the city welcomes each, if not for stardom then at least to show them the way!'

She looked around in wonder, scanning the streets and taking in the flow of life around her and after a long time, she really smiled, taking a deep breath of the air in which lingered the smell of the sea.

Reality struck! Hey, what was the time? 10:25. Oh My God, 10:25?! She was supposed to be in at 10 AM sharp. God, she was so late! She was about to rush in when she stopped, *Do I really want to go in?* She asked herself and stood thinking. And then, without much thought her lips curved in a slow smile, *the time had been scheduled for 10 sharp, right? Humph, why bother!* And then and there she made up her mind, and turned her back on it forever. "No looking back" she told herself. *It ain't easy but it's worth it.*

She went out into the street, smiling inwardly and was about to hail a cab when a speeding silver car abruptly stopped in front of her making her jump reflexively.

"Hey!" a familiar voice called out to her. Her heart skipped a beat as she looked into the face that she had so longed to see after all these days.

He was shocked too and literally jumped out of the car, "Hey, you know, I'm sorry," he said, looking around fearing that he was making a scene, "But I can explain." He was at a loss for words.

She was almost speechless and delightedly ran up to him, hugging him hard. They both held each other for a while, their quickened breaths calming and then both started talking at the same time, not making any sense.

"I can explain," he said finally.

"Yes, you owe me a great deal of explanation!" She exclaimed.

"I know," he smiled and just then it dawned on him, "But, but you had an interview?"

"No longer, I'm afraid!" She shrugged and laughed out loud and he joined in her excited laughter.

"So much drama!," He said.

"Yes, after all it is Mumbai!" She winked.

- x -

XXII

March is known for its winds, gushing, intruding and forceful. As such the whole yard was full of dry leaves and twigs after the windstorm late last night.

The house owner, although in the grasp of old age was a cleanliness freak. Unable to bear the mess all around, he himself got busy with a broom, sweeping his yard. He was engrossed in his task when suddenly he heard the squeal of brakes. He looked around.

A young man got down from the driver's side of a sedan. On observation, he seemed to be in his twenties. He was good-looking with fine features, lithe and somewhat tall, neither too lanky nor too bulky, he seemed fit. He had a fine sense of style which was reflected in his clothing, a leather jacket paired with denims. He opened the gate and walked into the old office building which housed a studio on the top floor, as the old man watched from his house opposite.

....

"So, someone is buying the studio?" Mr.Saxena said, sipping tea, sitting in the verandah of his house facing the same old building.

"Yeah, it's been a long time, but at least there's somebody who's come up and has agreed to preserve the studio instead of merging it with the office structure," said the owner of the building who seemed a sexagenarian.

"So you are leaving, huh?" Mr.Saxena said to his friend.

"Yes, I need to be with my family. They need me know, with Carla's demise and everything" Samuel Hardt replied and said, "What about you old friend, we've been together all these years."

"Yes, we have, the best of times and the worst," the other man smiled and added further, "but not me, you know that, I am staying."

So, in less than a week, Mr.Saxena's friend left his beautiful abode and moved to the United States and the old man was left alone to witness what was about to happen in their little studio of yesteryears. Maybe another young man had realized its importance and the magic that it held.

- x -

XXIII

Days flew like birds in the evening sky, and months passed like seconds in a clock, and seasons changed, soon it was autumn and the end of October. As the days became cooler with the blades of grass showing little dew droplets on them on early mornings, and the leaves turned golden brown, the festive season arrived. She was excited as this was the most colourful time of the year when the whole country dressed up in brand new bright attires and indulged in merry-making. Diwali, the festival of lights, illuminated the darkest of nights as myriad-hued lanterns and firecrackers lit up the sky.

Looking back, the past few months have had been the most hectic for her, but despite the rush, she had experienced some of the best moments, soon to be put up in selves framed as reminders of the past. The best part had been their joint effort. It had seemed dreamlike to her as they worked together, singing, writing, composing, talking, sharing and in the process making music; tucked away in their abode in the hills in the lap of nature. When a song was finalized and was being recorded, it was serious business, but the rest was about having a good time.

She felt as though they were living and breathing music, abandoning all cares and worries, indulging in just pure passion, and Lyla poured her heart and soul into it.

It was a long time since he had felt so happy. Eeshaan was doing what he had always wanted to do, and for once it made sense. It was no longer a loose end but a sensible means to an end, the end that was his dream of becoming a musician.

They had a vibrant team of collaborators comprising of a band, back-up vocalists, and DJs with *her* as the lyricist and *him* as the composer, singer and guitarist rolled into one. Plus, they had the recording team who had set-up office there. Basically, the crew comprised mostly of young people and they all had a good time, despite the serious business. There were problems, disagreements, dead ends and errors but their enthusiasm was always the last thread that somehow saved them from tearing apart.

They were venturing into a rather different genre of music; Eeshaan had jazzed up most of his past experiences together; there was an aura of country, tuned to rock beats and some punkish tinges altogether hyped up by a little dub-step.

....

The album was almost complete with only a couple of songs left, when they got some news. Sarah Anderson was in the picture again, the lady who had given Eeshaan his big break, and she wanted him to collaborate with an artist, a Russell Howard, who was an old client of their label's mother set-up in London. As she had put it, it would give him 'international exposure'. For that, they would need to travel to London in a week's time.

Lyla was pretty excited about travelling to the UK, as it would be her very first trip to the country and she couldn't help talking about it!

But Eeshaan did not quite favor the whole concept of travelling to London at that point of time. Yes, he did want to collaborate and understood that it was a great opportunity and a big boost, and totally appreciated Sarah's offer, but he was at a very crucial stage as they were about to wind up his Album and he needed to stay focused and concentrate on his music out here in the studio. He only wished Russel Howard would come to India rather than the other way round. But the real say was in the hands of the higher authorities, and eventually they were on a flight to London.

It was a two weeks stay. They had time for sight-seeing too. London with its glorious ambience and old world charm attracted her, and she fell in love with the sights and sounds of the city. But more than that she realized...*She had fallen in love with him.*

XXIV

Her love for *him* had blossomed in the peaceful aura
of the hills, in the midst of nature, away from the
complexities of city-life, *innocent and fragile*. She had
been so engrossed in making music together, so
caught up in his company and her admiration for
him that she couldn't recall when this admiration had
turned to adoration. She had been ignorant of the
strength of her feelings, which had finally found vent
when she was alone in London without him. Only
then did she realize how all this while she had been
totally in love with him.

Staying in that little hill-station, spending time in
such close proximity, she had been unaware of her
feelings for him, unaware that he gave her heart
premature ventricular contractions! His infectious
passion and the desire for good music that they both
shared, even perhaps his mere presence, all made her
tremulous heart skip a beat.

She had accepted the fact the she did like him a lot
and there were a few occasions of intimacy. But they
both took those moments of affinity as part of the
package, the strange undecipherable relationship that
they both shared. But more significantly it was the
connection that hailed from a sense of understanding,
an understanding based on a familiarity, that of the
undeniable imperfections that made them both

imperfectly perfect, against the odds.

But she had attributed it all to the fact that she really liked him and was more than happy to collaborate with him, writing songs that he so beautifully tuned to music. She almost felt the giggling schoolgirl notion of being in love for the first time as realization hit her, but was it the mere idea of love that enticed her? Or was it the reality of feeling it for someone that felt right, all by a sense of nascent familiarity. But Lyla was just too happy to even explore these complexities. Did I tell you that she found him undeniably attractive from the very first time they met? The chemistry was palpable right from the beginning, only they had both failed to see it, no wonder they kept coming back. Man, heavy stuff out here! But what about *him*? How did *he* feel about things?

Most disappointingly, there was a change in the air for them in London. In the beginning he was cross and she would understand, given the state of events. So she tried to cheer him up at the slightest chance, bringing in the same humour that they both swore by back in the past, but strangely enough he was uninterested. Rather he seemed to delve deeper into his misery or so she thought. He seemed disturbed, somewhat. She missed his easy grace and the spontaneous charm. He preferred solitude instead of company, her company, and she felt at a loss. It was as if he had shut himself in for some reason and she didn't hold the key to his cage.

He was so used to *her* presence that he was the most comfortable in her company. It was as if he could tell her anything, everything! She was always there when he needed her. Even in those low moments, just looking at her, at those beautiful kohl bright eyes that carried so much hope, so much faith in the extraordinary, would bring a smile to his face and keep him going despite all the madness around. It seemed she had more faith in him than he did himself. But all this was about to come to an end, the recordings were almost over and soon they would return to their routine lives. He was scared that it would be difficult for him to be without her. Eeshaan had never thought of love, it was too heavy-weight, and he was scared of the consequences, he was not used to it, it would be too big a risk. So he quelled such thoughts, if any. Instead he decided to concentrate completely on his passion i.e. music, blocking all else, slowly, ever so painfully letting her go. He would hate to hurt her. But what hit him most was the fact that he would more than hate to let her go, he could almost *feel* the void. These thoughts left him unsettled. He tried too hard to numb himself and felt the weight of it.

With him spending more and more time in the recording studio, she found solace in her solitary exploration of the city as she started to bestow her love upon it instead. She felt terribly alone and disappointed, and in these lone moments she realized how much she missed his presence and just about everything else. She was sad, trying to fathom the sudden change in his persona.

****

As the first flakes of snow touched the ground and winter beckoned, *she* left, vowing never to return. While abandoning it all, there were tears in her eyes but she wiped them away. Thoughts at this point were overrated, she was numb; for once in days, Lyla wanted to be back home.

He was both angry and sad at the same time. Eeshaan wanted to abandon all complexities and flash the truth, the absolute ultimate truth, but he could not. It was too late. Emptiness and a broken pride was all he had left.

. . . .

She drove away watching him diminishing in her rearview; only her car stereo had his record of love songs on repeat.

-   x -

WINTER

XXV

She was awoken from deep slumber by the rays of the morning sun shining through the window panes. The off-white linen curtains were half drawn; which was the first thing she noticed as she woke up. Through the glass she could see the makings of a bright clear day outside. Everything seemed calm and at peace, signifying a beautiful morning. Even the cobwebs shone in the sunlight and she was suddenly filled with a deep sense of contentment, some of it leftover from the night before.

As she turned over in bed, raising herself on her elbow and pulling her sheet close, she couldn't help but feel a heady concoction of emotions welling up inside her, as she looked with a mixture of admiration and something more, at the form lying asleep half covered, next to her. With his unruly black hair falling over his forehead, the perfectly curved jaw now covered by a stubble, and those beautiful expressive eyes shut, he was undeniably handsome. She longed to stretch out her hands and caress him as he had caressed her last night, his hands hesitant at first, exploring, finding, and then arousing in her such intense feelings as she had never experienced before. She in turn, had given up all inhibitions, and had delighted in pleasuring him in return. She had wanted their lovemaking to go on forever, and so had he, as they took each other to dizzying heights of rapture, fusing into one. The memory of it made her tremble in ecstasy.

While she was looking down at him, deep in thought, he suddenly opened his eyes and looked up at her, startling her and almost making her gasp, as she hurriedly tried to regain her composure. He narrowed his eyes at her reaction and smiled, and she smiled back, hoping that he had not read her feelings in her eyes. They continued gazing at each other, their eyes doing the talking as the memories of the night played in their minds. Outside, a dove cooed and there was a mixture of chirruping voices in the morning air mixed with the freshness from the swaying trees, and shrubs and bushes.

Time seemed to stand still in this wonderful afterglow. The two of them were totally caught up in each other, caught up in the gloriousness of nature! The alarm suddenly went off, breaking the spell, and they were gripped by a reality check. Reminded of their commitments, they went into a rush, and it was as if the symphony of nature outside too ended, as the creatures and plant life abandoned their leisurely bliss and engaged themselves in various activities for life and survival.

....

Somebody had once said, *poetry is alive in our day to day lives, if only we knew how to find it.*
'Maybe after all these days of seeking and searching, my life has been drained of poetry. No longer can I find songs in the ordinary.' She thought sadly.

On a similar morning, Lyla had been sitting in the airy verandah of her uncle's bungalow set amidst one of the sprawling tea gardens of Assam. The air was humid, the environment tropical and the scene around was green in all its essence, ranging from deep dark shades to the light softness of the new leaves.

It was April, spring in India, and in Assam, through which flowed the mighty Brahmaputra River, the season of "Bihu[4]" prevailed. The spring festival, Bihu, was marked by a vibrant plethora of folk songs, merry-making, dancing to the tunes of the 'dhol' and 'pepa' (traditional musical instruments), the locals dressed in 'saador-mekhala[5]' and the beautiful orchid

---

[4] Bihu is a traditional festival celebrated in Assam to mark the stages of harvest. The reference here is to the 'Rongali Bihu' which is held in April and celebrates the spring season.
[5] The traditional attire of Assam for ladies; a two-piece garment,

'kopow-phul' in one's hair!

The previous afternoon, a group of young kids, dressed in traditional attire, had performed on their lawn, singing and dancing to be rewarded with treats and money from her aunt. "'Hussori[6]' is still the tradition here", her aunt had said. Then there was also the feasting, the home-cooked 'pithas' and 'larus' and the countless local delicacies. So was also the exchange of hand woven 'gamochas[7]', adorned with skillfully crafted red flowers and patterns. It seemed as if the whole atmosphere was filled with a sense of celebration, a celebration of life and nature altogether.

The celebration all around made her happy somewhat but there was a void in her; as if her happiness was incomplete. As she thought about it, her eyes suddenly filled with tears. Before she could hold them back, memories came flooding in engulfed in hurt and the loss that wrenched her heart, and she succumbed to crying. With her relatives out for an invitation the empty house but for the cat, provided her the required space till she could pull herself back together again.

She remembered the first time they had made love. Maybe she had loved him even then. It had been out of the blue. They were sitting under the stars that night, warming themselves near the bonfire

---

usually hand-woven.

[6] A custom as part of Bihu where locales go around from one household to another, singing and dancing to bihu melodies.

[7] A significant hand-woven garment indigenous to Assam.

like they usually did on the weekends, as he strummed his guitar. Everyone else had left and they was simply sitting there, just the two of them, introspecting, not a word exchanged, when all of a sudden Eeshaan had spoken of passion.

****

He could remember it too. Something had been different that night. Amidst the silence, the bone-chilling cold, the aura of the blue mountains and the mystical hill tops around them, he was strangely drawn to *her*. Not because he loved her, as he did now, but maybe because he had wanted to feel, to touch, to explore, to soothe and be soothed, to lose himself for once in her warmth, but most of all he had wanted to experience passion. That raw physical passion, deep and alluring, that he had only heard of, the passion that defined art, yet that which he had never experienced in the right proportion, or in the right company. He had longed for it, yearned for it. And in a mysterious way that night, he had felt that she was the answer, the key, the means to an end.

He had tried to shake his head clear of these thoughts at that time. He was not even high! But when he looked at her, he couldn't hold back his thoughts anymore and spoke out his mind. Her eyes had also seemed to reflect the same longing, and she had agreed to indulge in the exploration with him. Looking back at it now, that night had been beyond words. The moment their lips had touched was pure ecstasy, and as they came together, their bodies had seemed to shatter into a thousand pieces in rhythmic unison, as though they complemented each other in a perfect blend of imperfections. He had felt himself lifted to another level of his existence, as though the cares of the world had fallen away from him. Much later, as she lay next to him with her head on his shoulder, he had fallen into a deep dreamless sleep, probably the best sleep of his life. He had not realized it then, but the next morning he had noticed something momentarily in Lyla's eyes, something that she had hurriedly hidden, something so pure and innocent that it had scared him, made him jump up, pack, and get out of the way as fast as he could! What a fool he had been!

-    x   -

XXVI

"I want to be a part of it, New York, New York!"[8]

He recalled Frank Sinatra's famous song as he walked down the city streets. Here in the Big Apple amidst almost 10 million people, he was a *nobody*. No, Madison Square had never even heard of him. The jostling Times Square, with its crowded side-walks and bustling life, added a certain kind of rush in him. There were so many people like him out here, all with big dreams in their eyes, setting out to make a mark. People from all walks of life, from all genres and flows of creativity, from all across the States, and even the world, were here, and New York City would make their dreams come true, or so they believed. No wonder, Bob Dylan too had found his true calling in this very city!

Central Park, Manhattan, Brooklyn Bridge, the Empire State Building, the Statue of Liberty, the Yankee stadium, the Grand Central Station and so much more and New York City was never boring. So, he had chosen to stay in this very city in order to regain his peace of mind, away from all the sudden fame and rapid change, and to rediscover his lost self and draw inspiration again. *Oh, for the love of New York!*

....

How long had it been? Six months? Since his first

---

[8] Frank Sinatra, "New York, New York", *Trilogy: Past, Present and Future,* 1980.

track went viral in India. Thanks to the Social Networking sites, the rest of the album was also well received. He had really managed to connect with the Youth, especially college-goers and people in their twenties and even thirties, all of whom needed a change from the usual stereotypes and his music had come in like a breath of fresh air. Eeshaan's album was sold out in a month! A first for someone so new in the industry! Now the music scene in India was somewhat different. But he could not forget those articles in the newspapers of him breaking records, setting a trend or something. Again, though the critics were a little too hard to please but at least they did not bash him up for being a newcomer. Strangely enough some had even used the words 'promising' and 'hopeful' and 'pretty good for a debut, definitely more than 'average '.

Within a month's time, Eeshaan was bestowed with an agent, who insisted on working on his image.

"See the big shots in the arena, to 'be them' you have to be like them." He would say.

This was followed by tiring schedules of promotions, attending events and even doing a commercial, *but the last experience had been so bad, that he swore 'never ever again'!* His good looks earned him a female fan base and his EDM- rock tinge went well with the boys. Soon, he began to receive invitations from influential social circles and found a place in the Page 3 scene. FAME! It didn't just pat him on the back, but completely filled his plate to overflowing and then too kept on pouring in!

With so much happening in such a short span of

time, he was overwhelmed and completely caught up in the moment. But as the days passed, he realized how hollow it actually was and also how miserably lonely and terribly exhausting! Eventually, the parties grew boring and the company tiring and excessive, and gradually he realized that there was much more on his plate than he had bargained for, and worst of all, that these were merely 'things', purely 'materialistic'.

The past few months had kept him so busy in his artificial, materialistic endeavors of fame and recognition, that he realized how he was no longer in contact with his friends and former acquaintances. At one point Eeshaan resolved, *enough was enough*, he seriously needed a break! So, he rented an apartment in New York for a month. He thought, NYC was what he needed right now,

"If I can make it there I can make it anywhere, it's up to you, New York, New York[9]."

....

After days of rushing and packed schedules that had eventually got the better of him, all of a sudden the stillness of the quiet, anonymous life he was leading in New York City brought forth a change in him, a little positive. He felt he could once again reconnect with his inner self and move back to normalcy after

---

[9] Frank Sinatra, "New York, New York", *Trilogy: Past, Present and Future,* 1980.

days of make-believe thanks to his sudden meteoric rise to fame, and it rejuvenated him.

But despite these moments of longing for peace, he felt a kind of void inside him. Delving deeper, it all went back to that last night at the hill station. Thoughts of the past triggered in him a memory that he didn't want to savor, because it made him feel as if he had *knowingly* done something wrong. No, he had taken the right step, or so it had seemed at that time, given the circumstances. It would never have worked out anyway. It was impossible. How could it? It had never been *love...or was it? He had never felt that way...or had he?*

....

Those warm bright eyes had mesmerized him the very first time he had met her in the Antique shop. Her 'inexperienced yet trying to be smart' persona, had appealed to him then, as had something more about her that had captivated him that day. He wasn't usually quite comfortable and open at first meetings but that evening he had found himself connecting to her at a deeper level despite the fact that there was not much talking. Maybe it was the silence, the quiet introspection and the talk about music and *belongingness.* And he was greatly awed when she had spontaneously come out with some lines in the middle of the street! Wasn't it cool?! The more time he spent with her, the more he began to like her company and he felt that music was the 'connecting link' between them, or was there *something more*?

Looking back now, his mind was filled with questions. All this while he had attributed it all to music and their love for it, the instant connection, the company, those moments of happiness, the fun, the friendship, the underlying element of love (*love*, there it was again) and support, the intimacy, the faith, yes, she had always been there. How could he be so ignorant when the signs were so damn visible! He had not even figured out his own *feelings* let alone reciprocated hers, while she had been brave enough to acknowledge them that day, and he had slammed them! How terribly he missed her now! Initially, he had attributed this realization to her absence and his loneliness. But then he realized that he actually *loved her*, yes he did, at least it was one thing he *was* sure of, because looking into his heart now he knew, Lyla was the *One* and there could never be anyone else.

But they had not spoken in months! There had been instances when he had tried to contact her, to apologize for his behaviour, much before this realization had even dawned, but in vain. Most of the time she was unavailable, God knew where she had gone off to!

In fact, he had missed her right from the moment she had left that day. In the beginning his own ego had gotten in the way when he had been foolishly blinded by fame. But now he no longer enjoyed the rapt female attention he received, and found himself unknowingly drawing comparisons. Only if he had realized earlier!

XXVII

The sun rays on the coconut palm made the leaves glimmer against the light blue sky. As she sat looking outside the window, she could see the golden beach almost deserted except for a random soul or two. It was midday and no one was out, thanks to the summer sun. Not such an ideal time for vacationing down South. But it was a much-needed break for her. She didn't feel like saying no for once in her life when her two really good friends from college insisted. "Why not spend a summer weekend together?" They had met, like after what, a year?

They settled for a quiet place down South, because just as Anamika had put it, "We don't want to be bothered by the crowd." And right now, right here, it was peaceful. Nature seemed to be in harmony with humans.

They were staying in a small yet fancy resort next to the beach with a great view of the sea, the waves heaving rhythmically, as if in sync with the very rhythm of life.

That afternoon as her friends planned some shopping at the local market, more of a sight-seeing trip, she decided to stay back on her own at the resort. After two days of hustle-bustle and travelling, she longed for some quietness, some time to just ponder a little, to weigh those *feelings*, to examine their status. Truth is, in spite of her self-repression, those feelings were still as strong as ever, but she had convinced herself that she was over him, which again she knew to be an absolute lie. She felt she would never be able to get rid of that unrequited hollowness inside her. She had thwarted all his attempts to contact her and had left on this holiday so that for at least a few days she could hide down here.

....

But that was not the only reason for her retreat. She had been aware and quietly observant of a certain new development in the past few weeks, before she had come away. Her father's best friend's family had become overtly connective with them. The two families had exchanged several visits and get-together parties, and had taken to attending events and ceremonies together. Most awkwardly and to her utmost surprise, on several occasions she had been thrown together and left alone with her old childhood friend, Arav.

He was the youngest of the siblings in his family, and she had grown up with him as they had both attended the same elementary school. But after that they had both gone their separate ways and had almost lost contact. He was an architect with a firm in Mumbai and only recently when he was home, had they reconnected. She could sense something fishy in the air, not on his part, but due to certain strangeness in the behavior of both their families. It seemed like they were trying to set them up together!

When this realization dawned on her, she was

initially horrified, but Arav on his part seemed okay with the concept. However, when she thought about it, she was aware that her family members were only trying to help her, given the recent state of events in her life. Oh no, no, they were not aware of her love tragedy, but they had seen her looking sunken and sad these last few months after suddenly giving up what she had so eagerly wanted to pursue, and they could only try to guess what burden was weighing her down. When she thought about it alone with her musings, hollowness welling up in her, she began to have second thoughts. She felt she had commitments which she needed to meet, and ignoring her suffering heart, she gave in to her calculating head, *just for the sake of it,* for the sake of her family? *Was it even the right thing to do?*

....

Lost deep in thought, she didn't even hear the door open, and the soft foot-steps, until her friend Kia lunged at her. She almost shrieked, "God, have you lost it?!"

"What the hell were you so deeply engrossed in?!" Kia asked, laughing.

"A penny for your thoughts?" Anamika said smiling.

"Oh, nothing," she smiling back; and then noting her friends' reactions, "Don't look at me like that, it's really nothing!"

"Oh wait," said Kia, the dramatic one, "Did you happen to meet some hot local, while we were gone?"

"Oh yes!" she said, getting the humor and they all

burst out laughing!

- x -

XXVIII

It was the busiest he had been since returning from his New York break. His country-wide 12 city tour was in progress. It had been quite hectic, living out of a suitcase, checking in and out of hotels and travelling, often flying from one city to another, *airports and hotels, concerts and the crowd,* he had never been so terribly alive and sickeningly tired at the same time! That night he was scheduled to perform in Shillong, the music capital of the North-East, and he was unsure of how he would be received there! He was more nervous than usual before the show, but to his sheer surprise and happiness, the show was a sell-out and the crowd welcomed him with love!

Driving along the winding hilly roads, wearing a sweater in the middle of July, he soaked up the peaceful feeling of a small town that belied its modern spirit. The verdant pine trees along the road and the post-card pretty houses with flowers abloom, was such a beautiful sight. *Shillong was such an underrated place when it came to Indian hill stations. Its vibrant ambience needs to be acknowledged,* he thought.

....

123

While on the drive back to Guwahati, looking out the window at the green hills with a waterfall or two in their midst, he began to think about the past few days. Immediately after getting back to India, he had tried to contact *her*. She had changed her cell phone number and he only had her land line number .But every time he called, he was told that she was out attending some event or the other and that she would call back, which she never did. The last time he had called before kick-starting his tour, she had gone off someplace else, out station! Meanwhile, Maya and Abhimanyu were no longer dating and were not even in contact. It seemed everybody was on the verge of separation! *Where was the connection, where was the love?*

After his failed attempts at contacting her, he grew both desperate and angry at the same time; he didn't know what to do! Meanwhile, his tour started and he engrossed himself in it, trying to cut it all out. *The solace of the nights lay in guitar strings and tequila shots awaiting sunrise.*

....

Eventually, after a lot of thinking and speculation, he decided it was best to give it some time. *Trust time to bring in the answers, trust time to heal.* However, his deepest fears lingered, that perhaps she had moved on… maybe, she didn't care anymore...He decided to give up. *Letting go was never easy.*

As days passed and time flew by, he tried to convince himself that he was over her, but in reality it was rather the opposite. Instead he kept looking out for her, for some sort of resemblance to her, in every potential girl that he met either casually or on a date, and was left further disappointed because they were *nothing like her*!

....

He drove away from the city streets and drowned in other attractions to cut it clean but only each night she governed his dreams.

She looked out the window and saw what she had never seen; everything in the universe reminded her of him!

- x -

.

SPRING

XXIX

Poor eagle, she thought looking up at the bird
circling above, no place to hunt for survival, the
habitat of its prey been cut down, the green cover
razed off by *inhuman* humans.   Everywhere she
looked was brown and barren; the sight was rather
sad, as if Nature had been deprived of its bare
essentials. Driving down the wide highway, with
nothing but concrete visible as far ahead as the eye
could see, those feelings of sheer loneliness
threatened to cloud upon *her*, making the journey
depressing all through. Lucy Schwartz crooning into
her ear, singing of life and the skies, was the only
occasional relief from the all pervading gray-ness.

She was driving at a higher speed than usual, as if seeking to escape from it all, as if to be done with it as soon as possible. Outside the window, everything seemed to pass by in a blur and she thought, only if life were that simple. The past was too hard to get away from, maybe because she didn't want to get away from it. She never could. *She loved him, yes she did even after all this time, and she was so sure of it that it hurt!*

Soon it was evening and the sky changed color; it looked like a splash of paint on nature's own canvas. The setting sun adding varied hues, golden, orange and red, to the clouded blue-grey sky and she sighed at the sight... Such beauty! The earth was beautiful.

She was to reach her destination by nightfall. It was to attend the *wedding*.

- x -

XXX

Phew! He was sweating even in the cool cabin of the airplane. He was in great hurry; no time to ponder over the clouds outside the window. His mind was preoccupied, and he openly ignored his co-passenger who tried to indulge in small talk.

From the moment he had grasped the news, he hadn't wasted much time as he rushed to pack and booked himself on the earliest British Airways flight to India. Checking his two-day old mail, he was horrified and his fears were further strengthened when his manager told him about the phone-call from some lady who had tried to contact him sometime back. He was certain, it was *her*.

He still loved her and perhaps she felt the same way too, the mail did seem to convey that. But she was getting *married* and that too *in less than 24 hours from now*! No! It could never happen! He was so very tensed, frustrated and sad, all at once.

It was a tiring flight, sitting motionless for so many hours, anxious, tense and awake. A tumultuous mixture of thoughts had clouded his mind throughout, and he felt jet-lagged as he landed at the Indira Gandhi International Airport that evening. It was getting dark and with all the lights on, the airport looked beautiful, but he had no time for that. As he collected his luggage and hurriedly walked out the exit gate, he could feel the interested stares from people around. He was famous in India, much more than he had expected. It was somewhat uncomfortable, but he ignored it altogether. A youngish man in thick rimmed glasses walked hurriedly towards him, taking his luggage and leading him to the car waiting for him. As he climbed into the back of the sedan, he felt he was still not used to this sudden fame.

He gave the chauffeur the address to *her* house, telling him to drive there as fast as he could. At this the young man betrayed a look of surprise which he quickly curbed, putting on the same neutral face that he had on earlier; it was not his place to question the change in destination.

The roads were congested and heavy with traffic, forcing them to slow down at times, and he couldn't help but constantly look at his watch. A quarter to ten! *Was everything over already?* That little thought was too painful to harbor and he tried to block it out.

....

At the somewhat old-fashioned single storey house in South Delhi, the old housekeeper was surprised to see a car stop in front of the gate. It was almost 10 p.m. and with his employers out, they were not expecting any guests. He switched on the front porch light and opening the main door, stepped out to see a figure walking towards the house with quick strides and stopping abruptly on seeing him. As the light fell on the visitor's face, the old man could see that it was a young man, with sharp, chiseled features that made him appear handsome; well dressed but weary, *as if he'd been traveling for long hours,* and with a look of anxiety on his face, as if he was in pursuit of something. They looked at each other in surprise for a moment, and then the old man spoke, "Hello. I'm sorry but my employers are not at home at the moment. But please come in."

At this he could see the look of shock on the young man's face, as he ran his hands through his hair and with a backward glance asked, "Are they at the *wedding*?"

"Why yes, they left this morning." The housekeeper said.

"Left?" He asked questioningly, but then realizing something said, "Where is the ceremony being held?"

"It is to take place in a resort in Assam, the day after tomorrow, to be precise," the old man informed him and then added, "Please come in and sit down."

"It is not today then?" He said more to himself than to the old man, and then remembering his manners added, "Thanks for the offer, but I've got to go now."

He turned to leave. The old man was rather surprised at the stranger's sudden visit, but he nodded his head and went in, closing the door after him.

- x -

XXXI

Kaziranga National Park, the place Nature calls *Home*.

Adorned in variety, the shades of nature prevalent, the dense tropical rainforest overarching the uneven landscape like a blanket of green garnered by trees, shrubs, bushes and grasslands and even swamps; nature things, each intricate and unique, of varied textures and content, appearance and form; nestled in the midst of blue hills, lush tea plantations and the mighty unstoppable

Brahmaputra, the place is sheer magic. Kaziranga is home to the One-horned Rhinoceros and countless other birds and animals, including the delicate deer, the magnificent elephants, the bored buffaloes and the freshwater aquatic life that abound in the Brahmaputra that flows by it.

The place was abuzz with tourists, especially foreigners, who generally put up at the many resorts in the area. The resort which they had rented for the weekend was a neat little place nestled in the outer circle of the forest, on the banks of a small tributary of the Brahmaputra, hardly bigger than a stream.

That night, the resort was decorated with colorful mini lights, lamps and paper lanterns, *glowing in the dark,* and there was even a bonfire. In order to maintain the serenity of the area, loud music and fireworks were strictly prohibited. A makeshift altar had been set up, decorated with wild flowers of different colors. There were not many guests, only the closest of friends and immediate family, who numbered hardly fifty. The wedding being a sudden affair, it was more of a secret event. The food was authentic Assamese cuisine prepared by the local chefs; and in keeping with the local tradition, 'tamul-paan' was served to the guests.

The bride was dressed in elegant Assam silk; a gorgeous pale pink shade with silver patterns along with silver jewelry and minimal make-up to keep up with the look; while the groom who was an out and out Assamese, was dressed as a typical, traditional Assamese 'Dora', white silk kurta and dhoti complete with the crown of basil leaves on his head.

After the ceremonies came to an end, the priest announced them husband and wife and both the bride and the groom exchanged rings and garlands.

....

Driving down the highway, he could see the scarlet-orange setting sun like a huge ball of fire in the fading blue sky. Soon darkness fell. The neon red strips painted on the road, illuminated by the headlights of passing vehicles, were the sole streaks of light along the way. It was a star-less night with a new moon and it seemed darker than usual. *The night was always darkest before dawn! Would it hold true in his life too,* he wondered.

The driver turned off the highway and drove down a narrow rough road for a kilometer or two and came to a halt near the entrance of what seemed like a large bungalow designed in indigenous Assam-type architecture, complete with the slanting thatched roof and bamboo walls carefully covering up the concrete. It was the resort.

As they drove in, a valet rushed to open the car door and Eeshaan climbed out quickly. As he rushed inside, he could see several people, all decked up and talking animatedly. His spirits sank a little but his heart raced as he looked around, he was half afraid of what he might see, *a married woman now?*

"Hello, son. Did you arrive just now? Please come and take a seat." Said an elderly man and pointed to the seating area. Before he could speak, another woman came in and said, "Oh you must be a friend. But you are very late, the wedding is already over. Do you want to greet your friends first?"

The wedding was over? He stood there transfixed, unable to move, unable to speak. Fear, cold and harsh, gripped him. He dared not think of the unthinkable. How could it have happened...?

"Hey *Lyla!*" The lady called out, "Please come here."

She heard her aunt calling out to her, and looking around saw her standing in the doorway with someone; the person had his back to her but in an uncanny way he seemed rather familiar.

He heard her name and as if on impulse, turned around.

"Yes, aunty, you needed something..." but she stopped mid sentence and was stunned completely, as she found herself looking right into the eyes of the man she loved, *and warm brown eyes melted into those deep black depths.*

....

The events that followed were much less dramatic than one would have imagined them to be, unlike the movies. She didn't immediately rush into his arms like she longed to do, nor did he give in to the strong urge to hug her hard. They both just stood there staring at each other, transfixed for a while, *never in her whole life she had felt so exhilarated and so terribly sad all at once and he stuck to that unfathomable reaction building within him a 'mixture' of odds, emotions and*

133

reality. Soon reality brought them back to their senses as the aunt questioned the strangeness of the situation.

The lady asked with puzzlement, "What's the matter Lyla? Why don't you take this young man to the newly-weds? He's a friend of theirs, he's reached just now."

"Yes, aunty..."She managed to find her voice somehow. It had all been so sudden that her mind filled up with turmoil of thoughts and feelings all at once, an amalgamation of surprise and shock. She even felt sort of numb; but one thing was very clear, deep inside she felt like her happiness was complete.

He didn't know what to say. He was totally overwhelmed at the turn of events. Had the lady just said that the newly-weds were some other people? Did that mean *she* was not married? God, she looked so beautiful.

It was hard to tear herself away from his gaze but she did somehow, and looked down before speaking, "Please come this way."

"Why?" he began to say, but noticing the lady looking at him questioningly, added, "Okay," and followed her.

As he came close, she felt as if a sudden jolt of electricity had passed through her body. She shivered involuntarily, blushing red. It seemed that he had felt something too because just then he took hold of her hand. She snatched her hand away, immediately regretting the move, and walked with shaky steps towards the altar where the newly-weds were seated, greeting people.

What were they doing? What was *he* doing? He hadn't come here to attend any wedding; he had come here to confess! And now when she was right here, they were going to meet some other people, strangers probably, and...

"Maya?" He blurted out, astonished to see her in full bridal attire. And then realization dawned on him, *oh my God!* Standing there, before him was none other than his best friend, Abhimanyu, the groom. It had been what, like months since he had been in contact with his best friends.

Somebody touched him on the shoulder. It was Arden. Eeshaan didn't know how to react, he felt both joyous and regretful at the same time, and went and hugged Abhimanyu hard. Jeff came and patted him on the back, and all four of them hugged each other, like in the past.

Standing next to Maya, Lyla looked at him in adoration. It was such a touching scene.

Eeshaan turned around to glance at her and saw in her eyes nothing but love. Suddenly, all the weight of the past few days seemed to fall from him and happiness filled his whole being.

- x -

XXXII

So many things were happening all at once. His best

friend just got married, all four friends were together again after such a long time; he was back in the country feeling like the earlier version of himself before the trappings of fame; and most importantly he was back with *her*. Yes, they were finally back together, talking and laughing again, but only as *friends*. It seemed she still hadn't forgiven him as she thwarted his every attempt that evening to talk with her alone, running away at every instance. He had wanted to grab hold of her and tell her everything, but for some reason he couldn't bring himself to do so. *Distance and space were both ugly metaphors.*

After seeing *him* there that night, all her pent up emotions had come back to her in a rush. She was so scared of the floodgates opening up, so scared of the anticipated consequences, the hurt, the pain, the possibility of the cruel past knocking at her door again, that she tried at every chance to stay away from him. She was afraid that if she was alone with him even for a moment, she'd lose her grip, blurt it all out, losing herself *again...*

He was here for his best friend. They were re-uniting after all this time. It was beautiful, seeing all the friendship and the love and she didn't want to stand in the way, so she too pretended to laugh and smile when they were together. Something inside her seemed to say, *"perhaps he is here for you"*, but she brushed off the notion, the thought was *too good to be true!*

....

After the ceremonial dinner, which everyone

relished, the talk and laughter continued late into the night. By and by, most of the older guests retired to bed, but the young people stayed up.

"I never imagined I would be getting married in the middle of a jungle!" Maya said.

"I always knew Abhimanyu would be into something like this!" Jeff laughed.

"Yes, yes, our hard core Nature lover!" Arden grinned, patting the groom on his back.

In the midst of all the conversation, Lyla suddenly noticed that Eeshaan wasn't there. Where could he be? The clock showed a quarter to 1.00. She finished her glass of wine and pouring some more from the bottle, finished it in one gulp.

"Whoa, easy on that girl!" Another one of her cousins remarked.

She gave him a neutral look and picking up the tequila shot in front of him, gulped it down too, following it with two more shots. Her cousin looked at her in astonishment. She ignored him. When she felt that she was sufficiently drunk, she got up and walked out through the glass doors onto the lawns. It was dark, with only a few lights here and there. She looked around to check if there were any signs of anyone nearby, and kept walking till she found herself on the narrow track leading to the water-front.

The river seemed rather peaceful in the dark, the light from the crescent moon adding an eerie glow to it. The night sky overhead was full of stars and the forest in the distance seemed unusually quiet. All of a sudden, she heard a soft rustling, as of foot-steps in the undergrowth on the opposite bank of the narrow river. She was so startled that she did not speak, but just kept looking towards the source of the noise. After a minute of two, she could discern a figure moving in the shadows. She was feeling light-headed but somehow maintained her resolve and kept staring. Just then something jumped; a slow delicate jump across the river, towards her. She gave a small cry and fell back onto the grass. She felt quite dizzy but managed to sit up. Looking closely, she cried out in surprise. It was a deer! A rather tall one, standing firm, its limpid eyes looking into her own! She sat very still. The animal waited, making sure that there was no sign of danger, then slowly and very delicately, it lowered its head to drink from the river. After a short while, it suddenly lifted its head, as if sensing danger, and then with quick dainty steps moved away, disappearing amidst the trees.

She found her voice. "I just met a deer! Oh My God!"

"What are you doing here?!" It was Eeshaan.

She turned around, "You won't believe what I just saw! A deer! Ha, ha, ha!" and she burst out laughing.

He walked towards her and tried to help her up. But she refused, tugging at his sleeve, saying, "What's the hurry about? Sit down, young man!"

"You are drunk. You better get inside." He said.

"No!" She held up her hands. "No, I'm not going anywhere!" And then shaking a finger at him, she started speaking, "You! You always have to leave, you have got to leave! Can't you just stay, for once?"

"I never..."He couldn't finish his sentence.

"You always run away from things. You are a scared little person! And look at me, the foolish one, falling in love with you! Hahahahaha, there it is! Oh my god, I just said, I love you, didn't I? God, the deer! The deer made me say it!" She started laughing again.

"Okay."

"Blame it on the deer! You know what, I'm done! I'm done hiding. No more!" She nodded her head, "You know what, I don't care, and I'm telling you that I love you, you got that? Good." Her voice trailing away, she passed out.

While he carried her to her cottage and put her to bed, he thought about the turn of events and couldn't help smiling. Let's spare the details for now. Don't worry; he didn't get into all the filmy action. But it had sure felt nice to carry her and then caress her hair before leaving.

....

"You never told me, man, that you were getting married." Eeshaan said to his friend.

"Yes, I did. But you've changed your contact details and got yourself a manager who probably knows every damn thing that's going on in your life, but chooses to cut out certain things so that you remain focused on your aim." Abhimanyu said.

"Yes, you are right. I have messed up a lot of things." He reflected ruefully.

"No you haven't. It's perfectly all right. It's just that you got a little loony with all the fame!" Jeff added mocking him.

"Yes, bitten by the bug, brother!" Arden said.

It was almost morning, with faint streaks of light beginning to colour up the sky, and the four friends just sat there.

"What really happened? Why the rush?" Eeshaan asked.

"You had probably heard about the break-up. Well, it's just that we finally realized that we were in love. We didn't want to wait and we also wanted to keep it as private as possible." Abhimanyu said.

Just then Arden asked in a curious voice,

"Eeshaan, What are *you* doing here? I mean, we never informed you about the venue, you knew nothing about the wedding, and as far as I'm aware, you were supposed to be in the UK, touring."

All three looked at him. Before he could say anything, Jeff asked, "Does it have something to do with, er, Maya's cousin? Wasn't she your songwriter or something? And wasn't she supposed to have got married two days back?"

"Yeah, Eeshaan?" said Arden.

His silence told them everything they wanted to know!

-   x   -

XXXIII

She woke up all of a sudden when her phone began to ring, but before she could pick it up, she missed the call. She rubbed her eyes, felt her head throbbing in pain; and checked the time on her phone. It was 12.30 in the afternoon! God, how she had overslept! Weren't they supposed to leave today? She jumped out of bed, but as she tried to stand up, she felt groggy and immediately sat down again and remained seated for a while. As she looked around the room, she could see a glass of orange juice and two Advil pills kept on her bed-side table. She wanted to brush her teeth first, but gave up the idea and swallowed the pills instead, hoping they would steady her.

Half an hour later, as she walked out of her room, she could see that it was a bright sunny day. The sunlight hurt her eyes, and when one of the resort staff, who was passing by, greeted her and asked if she wanted him to put up her lunch, she refused. She realized that she had drunk too much last night and now was suffering a hang-over. *Where was everyone? Had they left her behind? That would be ridiculous!*

She walked towards the main hall, hoping to find someone from the wedding party. If no one else, then at least she might find her parents, or even *him*. The thought of seeing *him* made her suddenly feel very good.

There were several other guests at the resort. A little boy was talking to his mother, and she heard him say, "Momma, there was a deer here in the resort last night! I want to see it!" His mother replied, "Sweetheart, it's not here right now, but you'll see lots of deer when we go on the elephant safari at dawn tomorrow."

"No, but I want to see the deer here!" He was persistent.

Lyla smiled to herself, kids will be kids! Suddenly, she stopped in her tracks. *Deer? Last night? Oh My God!!*

....

She needed to find *him*! Walking with quick steps, she searched for Eeshaan everywhere in the resort. What if he'd left already! He couldn't!

What had she blurted out last night? She wondered with a sinking feeling.

She was still dressed in her clothes from yesterday, and walking around in them was not very comfortable. She remembered how the night before, after her encounter of sorts with the deer, she had met *him* on the riverfront and had refused to go back into the resort like he had wanted her to do; but *what had she actually said to him?!*

"Ma'am? Hello ma'am." It was one of the resort staff who was calling out to her, hurrying to keep up with her quick strides.

"Yes." She turned around.

"Um, if you are looking for somebody, then here's a note that I'm supposed to give you."

She looked at him in surprise as he handed her the note. She felt as if she was living in the previous Century when there were only public phones instead of cell phones, and hotels often had to deliver paper messages for their customers!

142

"Ok, thanks."

Where was her phone?

God, what was up with everyone? *First, they leave me behind, and then they leave notes!* But she had to find *him* too. What if it was a note from him? She needed to find her phone first so she could call him. Oh, no! She didn't have his number! With this jumble of thoughts confusing her still fuddled head, she started walking back to her room, unfolding the note which read:

"After you rise and shine,
Meet me at the altar."

There was no signature on the note but she was certain that it was from *him*. But why, *'Meet me at the altar'?* Just then she realized that she was right there next to that very place, and turning around saw him standing at the altar. 'Now this is really dramatic!' She thought.

"I suppose you are looking for the others? I'm afraid, they have left already." He said.

"Yes. But they have left without me." She said.

"Yes. That's too bad."

"Eeshaan, why are *you* still here?" She was suddenly apprehensive.

He sighed, "I decided, I needed to *stay for once.*"

At this she looked at him straight in the eyes.

"You see, last night I was accused of being a 'scared little man'." He said.

This made her smile in remembrance and she

143

chuckled.

"Why are you standing here at the altar?" She asked smiling.

"Do you want to get married?" He asked seriously!

But before she could reply, she heard a scream and they both turned to see two teen-aged girls rushing towards them.

"Oh God, it's...it's really him!" One of them said excitedly.

"Are you real?... Yes, you are!" The other girl was incredulous.

He was so startled all of a sudden, that for a moment he seemed really nervous as the girls clamored for his autograph. Looking at the scene, it made her smile. She couldn't help admiring the man she loved, who had so unexpectedly, just proposed to her!

....

Though something inside her seemed sure, she still wondered if it really was *love* on his part, which had led him to propose.

While what remained of the wedding party had left by the evening, the bridal couple decided to stay on for a couple more days. Lyla too stayed back for the night, as did Eeshaan. Something still felt incomplete, as if there was some unfinished business between them. That night they were invited for dinner by the newly-weds.

Since their little encounter that afternoon,

circumstances had prevented them from having a proper talk. Somebody or the other had kept coming in the way! *'Tonight'*, he thought, deciding to finally give vent to his feelings. She too resolved, *'I must tell him tonight'*. It was getting difficult to hold back her feelings, with him so close. *It would have to be tonight!*

She dressed with a little extra effort that night. And as she walked out, she found him waiting along with their friends, leaning against his car. Her heart skipped a beat. In the pinstripe jacket over his crisp white shirt, and dark blue jeans, he looked super-hot! She couldn't help but sigh inwardly at the direction of her thoughts!

He kept looking at her for a moment longer than usual for she looked undeniably gorgeous in a golden mini wrap-around skirt and a black full-sleeved top with a bow in the back. *She is so beautiful.*

The four of them drove to another resort with a 5-star dining lounge; the place was crowded being a Sunday. Eeshaan was a little uncomfortable to be in the midst of so many people, given his identity, but he was put at ease by his friends and for once decided to forget about all the fame.

They had a great time. The food was delicious and the conversation kept flowing. Soon after dinner the newly-weds took off, and then it was just the two of them. Maybe it was a deliberate move on their friends' part, he couldn't help thinking.

She suddenly felt so damn shy! She didn't know what to say. They were both awkwardly quiet for some time, him staring at his phone and she looking around the hall. Smiling when they caught each other's eye and then suddenly, she spoke,

"How have you been?"

He was caught off guard by her direct manner, and looking into her eyes replied, "Not very good."

"Me neither." She said and added, "But why?"

"Ever since you left, I was never the same again. I'm sorry."

"You don't have to apologize. I understand how things stand."

"No, you don't. I have been rather foolish and ignorant." He said and added, "There's something, in fact, so many things that I need you to know."

She didn't reply but kept looking into his eyes, as if searching for answers.

"Do you really love me, like you said last night?" He asked, and she was so startled that she felt a psychological jump.

"I..I..what last night?" was all she managed to say.

"The truth, Lyla." He said, and hearing him saying her name in that soft, heavy voice made her shiver; "Why couldn't you have told me earlier? You have been avoiding me since I came here."

"So what should I have done instead? Why does it matter to you how I feel?" She literally shouted at him.

"Oh it does matter! Why do you think I came all the way from London, abandoning my tour? Just because I was so afraid that you were getting married and I'd lose you forever!" He replied.

"But why?" She was on the verge of tears.

"Can't you see why?" He said, almost exasperated.

"Oh, Eeshaan, please don't do this again!"

But before he could say anything more, a man came up to their table and casually and rather rudely, clicked their picture. Before they could protest, two boys also came over and started clicking more pictures. The restaurant staff rushed to their table and managed to drag the intruders away. This created a commotion and the other guests in the restaurant turned to look their way, some of them recognizing him.

She was irritated and stood up to leave. He thanked the manager and walked her towards the exit. The sight that met her eyes outside the door made her dizzy. There were camera flashes, as several photographers who were waiting there started clicking their photos and there was also some guy from the local news channel! The reporter came up to him with a microphone and started asking questions. It seemed Eeshaan was used to such situations. He calmly ignored them, saying "No comments," before holding her hand and leading her towards the car. But more people started arriving, perhaps to see what the commotion was about, and created a scene of sorts. The resort security had to come up and hold back the people, for them to reach their car. She got into the passenger seat and he took the wheel, driving away as fast as possible to hit the highway. It was rather dark, being surrounded by forests, but a beautiful night. They drove for some time without speaking. She was still upset and had not wanted to be in the car with him initially, but strangely enough, her anger gradually subsided, and she even started enjoying it.

He called somebody and said something about *'handling'* the situation that had just taken place. She thought, *was this the same person she had known a year back?* Maybe in his position, it did require him to have useful contacts.

Soon, they found themselves on the lane back to their resort and he brought the car to a halt in front of the gates. But before they stepped out, she spoke, her voice suddenly full of emotion, "Eeshaan, did you ever love me?"

Perhaps because of the situation that he had put her through that night, a part of his package, or the uncertainty in her voice, that he suddenly felt angry, and said something he shouldn't have. "Why are you even asking me this, after all this time?" He said, immediately regretting his words.

She stared at him for a moment dumbstruck, her eyes filling with tears, and then as quickly as possible she climbed out of the car and literally ran into the resort. He was quick to react, and followed her hurriedly, trying to keep pace with her.

As she entered the resort she saw several people around, which was rather unusual for a place like that, and she halted in her tracks. Everyone seemed to be staring at her and saying something amongst them, which made her feel like running away and hiding somewhere. Seeing her standing there irresolute, he rushed to her side and as if on an impulse, she turned and hugged him tight, clinging to him like he was her only refuge against the whole wide world. He hugged her back just as tightly for a while, and then pulled away so that he could look down into her face. And then ignoring everyone and everything around them, he kissed her in full-blown movie style, a long lingering kiss, his mouth on hers, seeking, searching, demanding, giving and she was engrossed in his taste, touch and smell; that seemed to say so much more than mere words ever could. There was no more need for him to declare his love for her, she *knew beyond a doubt,* and her impassioned response was his answer!

- x -

XXXIV

Dawn seemed surreal that day, a certain magical charm attached to the realness; a break from the mundane and life happened in real time. The first streaks of sunlight, serene and fragmented, lighted up the whole sky with a pinkish golden glow; the clouds looked like patches of illuminated cotton wool with a fiery lining, floating in the pale blue sky. It was a beautiful sunrise with an ethereal aura about it, and the sky looked as fresh and new as everything underneath; the blue hill ranges in the distance, the greenest of cover in the form of trees and fields, and the little ponds in the vicinity mirroring the morning sky. The leaves glistened on the trees, as did the dew spangled blades of grass, and in the distance far away, a billowing mountain of clouds seemed to beckon them, as though the road on which they were travelling led to paradise.

Travelling through the Kaziranga National Park surrounded by rare flora on all sides, the whole ambience was very picturesque. The dense tree-cover was interspersed here and there with large open areas of grasslands and swamps.

"Look, a Rhino!" She exclaimed, "Oh wait, there are more over there!"

"There are three of them and a little one too!" He observed, admiring the One-horned Rhinos that stood impressively still in their habitat, clearly visible from the safari trail.

They slowed down, hoping to see more wild life, and were greeted by a herd of deer who were grazing just beside the track. Not just the deer, there were also a few interesting birds which they couldn't identify, and some pelicans too.

Resuming their journey, driving deeper into the park, they saw some local people and an open jeep standing next to a spot with a sign-board that read, "Elephant Corridor", and much to their delight, they could see a herd of wild elephants at a little distance away, along with a few more deer close by! Looking up, they saw some kites and what was probably an eagle, circling lazily in the sky.

They slowed down and halted their car, to walk out and witness nature firsthand. Looking out into the distance, they were mesmerized. And as they stood there admiring the wildlife, they held hands, smiling into each others' eyes, sharing the thrill.

Something familiar which they mistook for large domestic cattle, were actually wild Indian Buffaloes.

It was pure ecstasy, witnessing nature at such close range, and having *love* as company! Free-flowing bliss seemed to pervade the morning air; turning it poetically charged with an undertone of music, and at that moment they felt that this was what was actually *living*.

As they drove into the early morning, they remembered their conversation under the stars last night.

The velvety black night sky had seemed to glitter, there were so many stars! The silence was peaceful, even soothing, as the deep greenery all around lay quiet, engulfed by darkness. The full moon glowed, pure and unadulterated. They were standing on the balcony, breathing in nature's silent beauty, soaking in nature's essence.

"Isn't this perfect?" He said, breaking the silence.

"Yes, it's beautiful." She smiled at him over her shoulder as she leaned with both hands on the railing.

He slid his fingers across hers, linking them. The touch of his hand made her tremble with pleasure.

"You know, like the perfect ending to something." He said.

"To what?" She looked at him questioningly, a smile on her face.

"To everything that we've been through, so far, to our story." He didn't know what else to say!

"But where's the sunset to walk into?" She laughed.

"Oh yes, pity, unlike the movies!" He laughed too.

She dissolved into giggles as he looked at her, a

mixture of emotions in his eyes.

She stopped laughing and looked at him, her eyes dancing.

"So, shall we seal it with a kiss?" He asked.

"How romantic!" She smiled teasingly, "The idea of you becoming romantic is so enticing". She added rather sweetly, "But no, not now. Let's wait till dawn for that."

"Are you sure?" He asked mock seriously, and she nodded. They were feeling playful, laughing, bringing in the humor, enjoying the moment.

Presently, the atmosphere between them changed and got somewhat intense. He put his hands around her waist and pulled her close at which she turned to face him, *the proximity igniting the flame*. Their bodies were touching, their breathing getting heavy. He looked down at her, an indefinable expression on his face and his eyes glittering. As if in response, she too looked up at him breathlessly, her eyes searching his.

"Why wait till dawn?" He asked, his voice husky.

"That's because our story has just begun. No sunsets, no endings, but a new dawn for us, a new beginning." She said, trying to keep her voice steady.

....

And that day as they had driven through dawn into the new morning, they had felt alive, as if they were born again, to renewed selves. The past few years, full of experiences, had been their making, and had brought them to what they were right then. The wide open road beckoned them onward, and as they looked through the rearview mirror, it was as if they could see their past fading away into the distance.

Setting forth on this new path full of beginnings, together, they indeed sealed it with much more than just a kiss. The song of their life was now replete with both music and lyrics, and that morning it lingered in the air, playing in their hearts, as they embarked upon a new chapter of their lives.

With hair blowing in the wind and smiles on their faces, they drove into the sunrise, as the sun peeped over the horizon, full of promises.

"I've never been up so early!" He smiled at her.

Sitting next to him, as she took the wheel, her hair flying, she smiled back.

Leaning in the passenger seat, he looked at her, his irises illuminating with pleasure and said, "But this moment, chasing sunrises with you in the highway, is something that I'll never forget."

Suddenly she stopped the car, with breaks screeching and an edgy turn to the side. He was overtly startled and looked at her with surprise as she removed her seat-belt and stared back, without a word. *And he remembered,* removing his own seatbelt, he leaned towards her, his hands in her hair and his mouth was on hers; her lips seeking, craving his, as he kissed her hard and long and they held on to each other for few minutes.

Later as she steered the car back into the road, she was laughing, as the taste of his mouth still lingered; while he put on some music on the car stereo, relieving her intoxicating smell on his skin; and Charlie Puth and Meghan Trainor crooned, "*Lets*

Marvin Gaye and get it on[10]"!

....

Taking things on a fresh wave, Eeshaan and Lyla travelled back to the little hill station to create a brand new album, with a set of songs all written by her. Meanwhile, their growing popularity as a musical duo, earned them many invitations to perform in some of the best locations all over the world. They traveled to the United States, Europe, halfway round the world to Australia, through Japan and South East Asia before returning to India to start the next trip to Africa! In spite of their respective individual endeavors, it was only when together that they created the best piece of music.

....

Well, like any other sucker for a happy ending, I should end this story with my favorite finishing lines from a fairy tale, *"And they lived happily ever after!"* But since I had not begun my tale with *"Once upon a time..."*, I would rather prefer to keep it realistic. Of course there were differences and disagreements, fights and the like, between the two of them from time to time, but soon they realized that it was all

---

[10] Charlie Puth Feat. Meghan Trainor, "Marvin Gaye", *Some Type of Love,* Atlantic Records, 2015.

about making it work, and as long as there's *Love*, well it just makes the entire process worth it.

THE END.

****

ABOUT THE AUTHOR

Currently based in New Delhi, Avilasha Sarmah is an alumna of Miranda House, and pursuing her Masters in Political Science from the University of Delhi. She is originally from the land of 'red river and blue hills', the aesthetically nature-crafted state of Assam, her home-town being the city of Tezpur along the Brahmaputra River, earmarked by tea plantations. Harbouring a love for travel, the author is drawn to mountains, especially the Himalayas, and has plans to travel the world. She loves writing travelogues tinged in poetic fervour, about the places and people that she embarks upon on her journeys. She is currently working on her second novel which is a fiction that depicts the conflicts and resonance in the yin and yang like notions of the yearning to travel and the comfort of a nest, portrayed in the story of two individuals.

The 23 year old author is a nature lover and is a supporter of environment and wildlife conservation causes. She enjoys nature photography. She is also a member of the Poetry Society India, (TPS) and has a blog: http://glittersenroute.blogspot.in/

She can be reached at:-

Instagram:
https://www.instagram.com/naturehues365/

Twitter: https://twitter.com/spideyas

Facebook:
https://www.facebook.com/avilasha.sarmah

LinkedIn: https://in.linkedin.com/in/avilasha-sarmah-910b3450